The Rose Red Reaper

Kristi Loucks

The Rose Red Reaper
Kristi Loucks
Copyright 2013 by Kristi Loucks

Editing and Formatting by BZHercules.com

ISBN-13: 978-0988723405
ISBN-10: 0988723409

Dedication

To Mom and Dad, for supporting me, even when I'm wrong.
To Bert and Annie, for reading through early on in spite of the
mistakes.

Kristi Loucks

Chapter 1

Mason Cole had spent the better part of a year trying to get over the scene that would be forever burned in his memory. The bloody handprint on the white tile in his bathroom, the size-twelve boot prints followed by a blood trail into his bedroom, and the sight of his girlfriend on their bed, arms tied over her head with surgically precise incisions gaping open from wrist to elbow on both arms.

Those were the visions that danced through his head each night, the visions that kept him from ever getting close to anyone outside of his brother Devon and his team: Piper Torello, an ex-SEAL like Mason, and Melinda Kade, who had been a technical analyst and profiler with the FBI before joining their Serial Crimes Unit in Chicago.

Each night, he went to the same place to escape his recurring nightmares, a little diner on Belmont. Mason liked it because it was within walking distance, quiet, and the waitresses seemed to understand that he wanted to be left alone, though it wasn't like the place was booming at two in the morning. Or at least most nights were quiet, anyway.

As he took his usual seat, he shook off the cold from the icy winter air. Within seconds of his arrival, a steaming cup of coffee had been placed in front of him.

He glanced up to thank the waitress and noticed the young woman sitting in the booth across the aisle from him. She looked beautiful with her long dark curtain of hair falling over her shoulder. Though he'd never spoken with her, she'd been there every night for the last seven months just like he was.

When he first saw her all those months ago, he'd just taken the position with Serial Crimes and moved to his new place down the road. He couldn't stay in the condo he'd shared with Jill for another minute after her murder. So, he'd found an old townhouse near Wrigley Field that needed some fixing up.

It had given him something to do with his time, since it seemed that time was all he had without her. Of course, after three or four months he'd pretty much fixed up nearly everything that needed fixing since Devon and Piper had helped out. Though Mason was pretty sure that it was just a way for them to stick close and keep an eye on him.

When there was no more work to be done, he'd started to walk around the neighborhood when he couldn't sleep. That's how he'd found his way into the diner to begin with. It was just underneath the red line of the El and surrounded by a number of late night bars and clubs that offered a place for the rowdier crowds to hang out. Mason wasn't a man with many vices, so those bars just didn't appeal to him.

On this night, Mason sat in his booth by the window, drinking his coffee and doing case research on his iPad, much like he had on any other night, reading every article that had even a remote connection to Jill's murder.

He was certain that her murder was not the first with the lack of hesitation marks or evidence in general at the crime scene. After almost nine months of research, he still had yet to see any signs pointing to a serial. But, that wouldn't stop him from looking anyway, because he was sure her murder was just an introduction.

After several hours of searching back issues of the Trib and Sun-Times, Mason scrubbed his hand across his face, letting out a frustrated groan.

"Not finding the answers that you seek?" he heard the woman say quietly from across the aisle.

"Excuse me?" he asked, not certain he'd heard her at all.

"I said, are you not finding the answers that you seek?"

"Oh. I guess not," he answered as he shut off his iPad and set it aside.

Mason stood up and walked over to her booth holding out his hand to her. "My name is Mason. Mason Cole, but most people call me 'Mase.'"

"Dakota Rose Shelton," she said as she turned in his direction. She looked right at his extended hand, but made no effort to accept it.

"You have something against shaking hands?" he asked, feeling a little embarrassed as he continued to hold his hand in front of her.

"Nope, just didn't know one was offered," she said as she raised her gaze to his. She stared through him with the bluest eyes he'd ever seen, but they didn't focus on the hand he'd extended in front of her.

"Retinoblastoma. I've been blind since I was four years old," she said as she held her hand out towards his still outstretched hand.

Mason caught her hand in his and started to ask if he could sit, but she spoke up before he had the chance.

"Please don't apologize. Everyone always does that," she said.

"I was just going to ask if you'd mind some company. Seems we both spend an awful lot of time here. Alone," he said with a laugh.

She smiled and waved her hand in front of her by way of invitation, so he took the empty seat across from her.

"Can I buy you a cup of coffee?" he asked.

"Sure," she said. "Judy, can we get a topper?"

"Coming right up, Miss Dakota," the waitress said as she came over with the carafe.

"So they know you by your first name around here?" Mason asked.

"I would hope so, I sign their paychecks." She laughed.

"Huh, so you own the place? I guess that explains why you're always here then." He smiled.

"Yes, so what's your excuse?" she said with a smile.

"Please don't feel the need to beat around the bush or anything," he teased, wondering how she knew he was there every night.

"What? You don't think anyone's told me that Mr. Tall, Dark, and Broody was here every night?"

"I suppose they would." He laughed. "Tall, dark and broody, huh?"

"Pretty much. Oh, and gorgeous. They told me that you were gorgeous."

"Wow. Are you this straightforward all the time?" Mason asked.

"Well, when I don't have to see the look of shock on your face, it's pretty easy." She smiled. "Besides, there is always a chance that they could have been lying to me."

"Maybe they did," he said as she started to laugh aloud.

"I doubt it. I can hear the way people talk to you. It tells me a lot."

"Like what?"

"Well, women coo at you and when you give the clear back-off vibe, it only deters them for a couple of minutes. If you were unattractive, they wouldn't be as persistent or more likely wouldn't have approached a stranger at all. Plus, Judy's daughter, Colleen, came in a couple of weeks ago and said you were a 'hottie.' When I asked her to explain, she told me you had dark hair, heart-stopping blue eyes, were tall, strong, and had some seriously sexy ink. Usually when she describes men she says 'he's cute,' so I knew you had to be above average to warrant such an elaborate description." She smiled.

"Hmmm. Well, be sure and tell Colleen thanks for the ego boost." Mason said.

"Why do I have this feeling that you are rarely in need of an ego boost?" Dakota asked with a bright smile.

"Probably true," he said as a smirk swept across his face.

Just then, his phone beeped. "I have to take this. It was really nice talking to you, Dakota. Maybe we could do it again sometime?" he said as he reached out and allowed his fingers to touch hers briefly.

"I'd like that."

Mason stood and picked up the call as he set a twenty on the table under his coffee cup.

"Dev, it's almost four in the morning. What's going on?"

"Mase, I think we have another one." A chill ran down Mason's spine as he grabbed his stuff and headed for the door. He wanted to wave at Dakota, but obviously, that wouldn't have been very effective. So he waved at Judy, hoping she'd relay the message for him.

"Where?" he asked.

"Montrose Harbor. Condo. I'll text you the address if you want, but I'm about two minutes from the diner. Want me to pick you up?"

"How'd you know?"

"Mase, I'd have been shocked NOT to find you there," he answered.

Mason hung up and stood in the alcove, away from the blistering cold air that whipped by the old building until he saw Devon's Silver Ford Edge pull to the curb. As he walked over, he glanced back through the window at Dakota and saw that Judy had settled into his seat and was smiling at him as they talked. Once Mason was settled into the passenger seat, he noticed the glance that Devon shot back towards the diner. He was busted, and he knew it.

"Shut the door! It's freezing out. And what's that wistful look about?" Devon asked as he poked Mason in the ribs.

"Nothing. It's nothing. Tell me what we've got," he said as he slammed the door, effectively ending any further discussion about the diner or its owner. Devon turned on the flashing lights and shot out in front of an approaching cab.

"Brunette, twenty-six years old, green eyes, slight build. Julianne Howard. The husband, Ryan Howard, called it in. He's a pediatric surgeon. He was on the graveyard shift tonight, so he found her when he came home from work."

"What makes you think it's our guy?" Mason asked.

"The medical examiner was called immediately. I'm guessing something stuck out when she arrived because she had the officer on the scene call Captain Taber. I don't know why yet, but Dr. Hovey wouldn't have asked for him to call us if she didn't have a good reason. Good enough that she persuaded Taber to call us in without hesitation."

They rode the rest of the way in silence. Devon pulled up in front of the building and the two of them headed into the lobby, flashing their badges as they passed.

As they entered the main lobby, Mason quickly surveyed the room until he found a distraught man in his late twenties surrounded by two medics and a number of uniforms. "Mr. Howard, I'm Lt. Commander Mason Cole and this is my brother,

Detective Devon Cole," he said as he held up his ID and badge. "I'd like to ask you a few questions if you're feeling up to it."

"It's Dr. Howard, and I've been over it a dozen times already. I'm not sure what I can tell you that I haven't already told the others," he said as he stared vacantly across the room.

"I understand that it seems redundant, Dr. Howard, but I'll only be a minute."

The man gave a slight nod and Mason knew it was the only affirmation he was going to get. "What time did you get home tonight?"

"Around 3:00 a.m. I work at the Children's Hospital. I was on graveyard tonight," he whispered towards the floor.

"And your wife, Julianne; what time did she typically get home?"

"She works . . ." He faltered and choked as that reality sunk in. ". . .worked as a vet's assistant. She gets home around 3:30 p. m. Oh, God, she was still in her scrubs. Was he waiting for her?"

"We're not sure, but we're pulling all of the surveillance footage from the common areas. We're doing everything we can to find out how your apartment was accessed and if anyone suspicious has been spotted by the surveillance cameras," Devon said as he pointed to the security guard, who was boxing up DVD's for one of the uniforms near at the front desk.

"I know this is tough, but can you think of anyone who might have held a grudge against you or your wife?" Mason asked.

"God, no. Julianne was the kind of person that set everyone at ease and I'm a pediatrician. We help people," he answered, seeming baffled at the idea that anyone would target them specifically.

"Is there anyone you can stay with for a few days? Siblings, Parents?" Mason asked.

"My folks are on their way down from Madison."

"What about Julianne? Would you like us to notify her next of kin?" Devon asked quietly.

"No. I'm all the family she has," Ryan Howard stated.

"Okay. Well, Officer Galen is going to take you to the station to wait for your family. We'll be in touch if we have any more questions for you."

"Will you let me know when you catch this son of a bitch?" Ryan asked.

"We will," Devon said as he stood and waved Officer Galen over.

"Unit 17-D. Torello and Kade just went up," the officer said quietly to Devon as he moved to help Dr. Howard out to his vehicle.

"Mase, are you going to be okay with this?" Devon asked with a heavy dose of concern in his voice as they rode up to the seventeenth floor.

"Don't know," he answered honestly, as a ping signaled their arrival on the seventeenth floor. When they entered the hallway, Mason spotted Torello and Kade immediately. Piper looked like he was about to add to the body count when the officer at the door wouldn't let him pass.

"Come on, buddy, just call it in. It's our scene now," Mason said as he flashed his badge at the rookie cop. The kid was looking just a little green around the edges, so he knew it wouldn't take much to get him to hand over the scene.

Of course, the kid immediately called in only to have his supervisor confirm Serial Crimes had the case now. A look of relief passed over his face before he managed to conceal it once more.

"Sorry, sir. Go on in," he said as he looked at the ground.

Mason went first as he pat the kid on the back and Devon trailed in, hot on his heels. As they entered the room, the responding officer made a quick exit, being careful not to disturb any evidence on his way out.

The first thing Mason saw was a trail of blood that started at the bathroom door to the right of the entrance, leading into the living room. Fifteen feet in front of him was Julianne Howard. According to her husband, she was twenty- six years old. She had long dark hair and her green eyes were staring lifelessly through him. His heart rate picked up as he looked at a pose that had become so familiar to him, if only her hair had been blonde and her eyes hazel. Regardless of their different appearances, it was hard not to draw a comparison to Jill, given the similarities surrounding Julianne's murder.

Her hands were strung tightly above her head and secured to an old radiator with duct tape. He could smell the faint odor of burning flesh and adhesive. It was nauseating. Worse was the pungent coppery tang of blood and there was plenty of it splattered around the room.

This time, the killer had planned his timing better. Unlike Jill, she had been alive when he made the first cut. It was clear that her blood was pumping rapidly as she'd bled out. The same precise incisions, only this time blasting nearby surfaces with arterial spatter. He cringed as he looked at the same boot prints on the floor. Size twelve work boots with heavy lug soles, it appeared. Though this time, he had sliced from groin to kneecap straight down the femoral artery and carefully placed tourniquets on each leg in order to ensure he had plenty of time to enjoy her life spilling out before him. They had been placed before the cuts had been made, no doubt, and tightened to slow the blood flow after the first cuts, judging by the distance on the spatter. She had been tied tight and forced to watch as he bled her dry.

A single white rose petal floated on the dark sea of blood that was beginning to coagulate in front of the victim. Mason glanced around, looking for the rose that had shed the petal, but there was none to be found.

He ran his hands roughly through his hair as he listened to the shutter click with every photograph Piper took, while Melinda placed evidence markers around the scene. He looked at Devon and signaled towards what he'd assumed to be the bedroom, and the pair walked down the narrow hallway, following the boot prints once again. The same way he'd followed them through his own home as they led him to Jill's body. His heart pounded as he got to the doorway and gently pushed the door open.

As they entered the room, Mason noticed three boot tracks that grew fainter with each step the killer had taken as he walked onto the pristine white carpet. They led right to her dresser where the killer's calling card stood on the dresser. The fluttery click of the camera drew Mason's attention as Devon photographed everything before they entered the room.

Alone on the dresser sat a bud vase with two white roses in murky pink water, blood dripping down from the petals like confetti onto the surface of the pine dresser.

Upon closer inspection, they saw a small white envelope tucked against the thorns and leaves. A single drop of blood clung to the stark white envelope, blooming outward as it saturated the fibers.

Devon slid the flap open and gave it a shake, letting it flutter into Mason's gloved hand. As it fell free, an ID card slipped to the floor. Mason bent to pick it up and felt the oxygen rush from his lungs as he turned the card over. The woman who had haunted his dreams was staring back at him; the ID had belonged to Jillian Stroh. His hands shook as he handed Jill's ID to Devon.

"Son of a bitch!" Devon said. "Guess he didn't want to leave any doubts that he was responsible for Jill. What does the message say?"

"Roses are Red," Mason said as he showed the card to his brother.

"Is that blood?" Devon asked.

"I think so, and it looks like he wanted to make sure he had our attention," he answered as he flipped the card. It had been signed on the back, too.

ROSE RED REAPER

Chapter 2

"Well, I guess we know what to call him. The press is going to have a field day with that one," Devon commented.

"Which is why we need to get ahead of this and keep it out of the press for as long as possible. You know if the media gets a hold of it, people will go into a panic."

"What are we trying to keep out of the press?" Melinda asked as she and Piper entered the bedroom.

"This," Mason stated as he handed the calling card and Jill's ID to her after slipping them into evidence bags.

"These roses aren't red." Melinda said before inspecting the blood that dripped from the petals and saying, "But, I guess they are when he's done with them."

"And he certainly isn't squeamish about blood, is he?" Devon asked.

"The press will definitely eat that up if they catch wind of it. He's not fooling around. To say he's escalated would be a gross understatement. This wasn't a quick kill," Piper said as he turned the evidence bag over in his hand.

"What's he been doing all this time? It's been almost a year. That's an eternity for a serial to wait between kills," Melinda said.

"I've been over and over every neighboring state and found no evidence that he's been active within five hundred miles in any direction. Mel, we're going to need to open up the search parameters. Widen the net; maybe he's a transient worker? There has to be something we're missing," Mason stated.

"Sure. I'll get on it as soon as we catalog the evidence we've found here. And we'll start trying to connect the dots between Jill and this victim while we're at it," she answered.

"Maybe he was looking for something?" Piper guessed.

"Well, it looks like he found it," Mason said as he looked around the room.

"I guess his 'name' is pretty easy to figure out, given the roses and the blood," Devon added.

"Could have another meaning though. There's no point in canvassing florists since every single one will have sold dozens of white roses on any given day. Either way, we'll have to check credit cards, her job, places she visits often, memberships to the gym, everything. We need to know what a day in the life was for Julianne Howard and how she could be connected to Jill. If there is a connection we need to find it!"

A couple of nights later, Mason sat at his kitchen counter with pictures of Jill and Julianne littering the surface. A few with bright eyes and smiling faces, but more that told the grim tale of how they had spent their last moments on this Earth. They'd found no immediate connection between the two woman, but Mason was certain they had not been selected at random. Their murders felt far too personal for that.

It was hard not to wonder if Jill had cried out for him. Hoping that he'd come home early. That he would save her. So many times, he'd been jolted awake, hearing her scream his name, begging for him to save her. So often, that it took only a little more than a thought to conjure what he thought her last words might have been in his head. Not even a nightmare to prompt it anymore.

His phone rang as he stood abruptly, knocking the stool he'd been sitting on to the floor.

"What?" he yelled into the phone.

"Ease up, man. I just called to see if you wanted to grab a bite to eat. Get out of the house for a bit. Maybe we could go to the diner?" Devon asked.

"Sorry, Dev. I didn't mean to yell. I'm fine really. You don't need to babysit. I'm just going to go out for a run," Mason lied.

"Okay, well, if you change your mind, you know where to find me. If not, I'll see you in the morning. Want me to pick you up around seven thirty?"

"Sure. That sounds good. I'll see you in the morning," Mason said as he disconnected the call.

After a few more minutes of looking through crime scene photos, Mason decided to go for a run after all. Then maybe he'd stop off for a cup of coffee on his way back.

There was nothing like the cold Chicago air to make you run a little faster. But, at least the diner wasn't too far from his place, so the run home wouldn't be nearly as long as the trek he'd made around Wrigleyville before stopping off.

The bell over the door rang, alerting Judy to his presence. He glanced around and noticed that Dakota wasn't there. For the first time in quite a while, disappointment registered as he resigned himself to sitting alone. Mason went about peeling off the extra layers and set down his iPad, which he had carried with him. He was suddenly glad he hadn't left it on the counter.

Judy arrived just as he'd taken his seat and placed a steaming cup of coffee in front of him. "Here you go, doll, just let me know if you want a refill."

"Thanks, Judy. I will," Mason answered as she returned to the counter and picked up her newspaper.

He turned on his iPad and started to look through various emails from the Medical Examiner and his team regarding Julianne Howard's case.

After about twenty minutes, he swiped a hand over his face and sighed in frustration.

"Thought this might help warm you up. Judy said you looked like you'd been running. Didn't you get the memo that it's winter?" Dakota asked as she set a plate with a piping hot cinnamon roll down on the table. She let her hand slide across the back of the booth to guide her ascent as she sat down across from him, setting her own cup of coffee carefully on the table. "I'm sorry, I should have asked if you minded some company."

"You know, I may not be too mindful of the dropping temperatures, but I'd never turn down the company of a beautiful woman."

"Well, that was about the sweetest thing anyone's said to me in a while."

"Been hanging around with the wrong kind of people, then. Thanks for the cinnamon roll. This looks amazing. Now that you're here, you can save me from having to run the long way home by helping me eat it!" Mason said with a laugh.

"Sounds like a good idea. Wouldn't want you to have to spend more time in the cold than necessary," she said with a smile.

As he took the first bite, it was impossible not to let his eyes close and let the groan of satisfaction escape. It was quite possibly the best thing he'd had since he was a little kid.

"This is amazing! Do you make these here?" he asked.

"Yeah. I make all of our breads and pastries. You just happened to come in when I was finishing the batch for tomorrow morning. So I pulled one off the tray before it went in the fridge and put it in the oven for you. Judy said you looked like you'd had a rough night," she said as she took a bite.

"She did, huh? Truth is I could use a pick-me-up. But seriously, you make all of the pastries? And here I thought you were just the brains behind the operation. This is really good, by the way. I may have to swing by and pick up a dozen in the morning; my brother and the rest of my team will go crazy over these. Can I place an order?"

"Sure. What time do you want to pick them up?" she asked.

"Around seven thirty? Is that okay?"

"Absolutely. Would you like some coffee, too?"

"That'd be great. The stuff they make down at the station is like drinking motor oil," he answered.

"So, you're a cop, then. I guess that explains the late night calls and the weight of the world you seem to carry," she observed.

"Not exactly a cop. I'm actually Navy, an ex-SEAL, but my brother is a detective and we were called in to head up a Serial Crimes unit."

"Wow. So how'd you end up in Chicago working serial crimes?"

"I grew up in the area, did my training at the Naval Base in Grayslake, and my brother, Dev, has been with Chicago PD for about ten years. When I came back, I was planning to work at the Naval Academy, but then something happened and I changed my plans. Let's just say that I have a vested interest in the unit. I'll spare you the gory details though. Anyway, that's how I ended up with the job," he offered as they continued to pick at the cinnamon roll.

He could see her mull that over, but eventually she let it slide, probably deciding he didn't want to tell her, which was only half true. It was more that he feared the truth would scare her off, but he wanted to tell her and that was a first.

"You and your brother must be close. That's nice. So, ex-SEAL. Didn't know there was such a thing."

"Fair enough. I'll always be a SEAL, but I'm not on active duty. Sometimes it's just easier to explain ex-SEAL. Anyway, I finished my third tour a little over two years ago, and I'm needed here now. And yes, despite the fact that he worries too much and can't stay out of my business, we're pretty close."

"So, what brings you by tonight?" she asked.

"Well, I was out for a run, and I decided to stop in on the way home. I like the company," he said quietly.

"Me, too," she replied as she set her hands on the table in front of her.

Mason reached out and put his hand over hers as he said, "I really like talking with you. How about you tell me something else that I don't know about you."

"Well, you know that I love to bake, and that I own a diner. Hmmm, I grew up in Southern Wisconsin on a farm. I love baseball, and I'm a die-hard Cubs fan."

"Thank God you're a Cubs fan. I thought I was going to have to find a new diner to frequent if you said you were a Sox fan," Mason said with a laugh.

"How about you? What makes you tick, Mason Cole?" she asked.

"Well, aside from being a cop, a SEAL, and a brother...Dev is going to love you when he gets his cinnamon roll in the morning, by the way. Let's see, something you don't already know..." He thought for a minute before adding, "I love to cook, but I can't bake at all. Oh, and I have a degree in Criminal Psychology."

"Wow. Good looking and intelligent. I guess that explains the leap into law enforcement, too," she said.

Mason laughed at her comment. "Yep, but my brother would probably also tell you that I'm an adrenaline junkie, I act without thinking and that I can be a little reckless."

"Is he wrong?" she asked.

"Hmmm. Usually not, but don't tell him I said that. He'll never let me forget it," he said as he finished off his coffee.

"Would you like some more coffee?"

He looked at her, a little stunned. "How'd you know?"

"The cup sounds different when it hits the table if it's empty." She smiled as she waved Judy over.

As Judy topped off the coffee, Dakota gave her the order for the next morning.

"I'll put it in the system, hon," Judy answered before turning to Mason. "Molly will be on in the morning, I'll make sure she has everything ready to go at seven-thirty sharp. Anything else, doll?" the older woman asked.

"No, I think that'll do it, and thanks for tipping off the chef," he said with a wink. "I knew there was a reason I liked this place. Great service, great company, great coffee, and now there's the cinnamon rolls." He smiled.

"Oh, and here I was thinking it was just Miss Dakota," she said as she walked back to the kitchen.

Dakota put her palm to her forehead as she shook her head in embarrassment, until she felt Mason's hand close around her wrist and pull her hand back into his.

"Don't do that. I know we haven't known each other very long, but I really like talking to you. That blush that's coloring your cheeks, I think it's coloring my cheeks, too," he said as he placed her hand against his cheek.

She smiled as she felt the warmth under her fingers. "Well, at least I'm not alone in my embarrassment, then."

Her fingers tingled as she felt the rough stubble on his cheek and neck. She noticed the defined angle of his jaw and the calluses on the hand that held hers against his cheek.

"You do a lot of work with your hands?" she asked.

"I like to do renovations. Mostly on my house or my brother's. It's what I do when I can't sleep, well, what I did. Seems there are no more renovations to be made. I considered flipping the house to start over, but I fell in love with it so I had to find something else to do. Now I come here instead."

"I'm glad," Dakota whispered.

She could feel a dimple in his cheek as his lips curved up in a smile. Her thumb slid over his full lower lip before she pulled her hand back as she felt him shudder and she quickly said, "I'm sorry, force of habit."

"It's okay," he said softly. "It's getting late; can I walk you home?"

"Sure. It'll be a short walk. I live a couple of blocks from here. Let me grab my coat and tell Judy that I'm leaving."

He stood and pulled on his jacket as he watched her move behind the counter to tell Judy that Mason would see to it that she made it home. Once he'd gathered up his belongings, he picked up their coffee cups and the plate and carried them over to the counter.

"Well, aren't you a peach," Judy said as she winked at him.

"The least I could do. How much do I owe you?" he asked.

"It's on the house," Dakota said as she walked back towards what he assumed was her office.

"No, ma'am. And Judy, I'll pay for my order, too," Mason said.

"That'll be $15.32, then," Judy told him. Mason handed her a twenty and shook his head when she reached in the drawer to pull out his change.

"Keep it. I mean it." He smiled.

Judy shook her head and said, "Thank you. And thank you for walking Miss Dakota home. She likes to do everything for herself, but I worry about her walking home at this hour."

"I'm happy to do it, plus it gives me a few more minutes to talk to her."

They both smiled.

When Dakota returned, Mason helped her put on her coat and hefted her computer case over his shoulder as he looped his free arm through hers.

"Where to?" he asked.

"I have an old townhouse a couple of blocks from here. Follow me," she said as she pulled a folding white cane from her computer bag, which hung from his shoulder.

Mason watched as she used the cane to assess the terrain in front of her. He suspected she knew it quite well, but in a big city, you can't always count on your surroundings staying the same from day to day, especially near Wrigley, which seemed to be under a constant state of construction even in the winter.

"How long have you owned the diner?" Mason asked as they walked.

"Almost five years now."

"And have you always baked everything in-house?"

"Yes, my mother loved to bake. Mostly, I fell in love with it because it was something that I could rely on solely by feel. I didn't have to see the dough to know that it was ready," she answered as she let her free hand coast gently over the iron fences on this particular block.

"I can see how that could be an advantage. Still, it's kind of amazing," he told her.

"This is mine," she said as they got to the front steps. "Would you like to come in and warm up?"

"No, that's okay. Maybe another time, though. Can I walk you to your door?" he asked.

She laughed quietly and said, "Sure. Such a gentleman."

"I swear my mother would haunt me for eternity if I wasn't. But, I just want to make sure you get in okay before I head off," he said.

She unlocked her door and stepped inside. He noticed she didn't switch the lights on before realizing the lights wouldn't have an effect on her ability to "see" anyway. "She's been gone a long time? Your mother, I mean."

"Yeah. She died when I was sixteen. My dad took care of us until he passed away when I was eighteen and Dev was nineteen. I went straight into the Navy after he died."

"I'm sorry to hear that. Both of my parents were killed when I was ten," she told him.

"I'm sorry. That had to be tough."

"It was. I don't think that kind of thing is ever easy whether you're ten or eighteen," she answered.

"I suppose that's true, but I'm sorry all the same," he said. "Did you have other family?"

"I had an aunt who lived in Chicago. That's how I ended up here, I guess. I lived with her and her husband until I turned eighteen. They used to run a diner down on the Southport."

"You got along, though?"

"Yeah, we got along for the most part. Our opinions differed on how I would survive in the 'real world' as someone with a handicap. Of course, I don't see blindness as a handicap, but she did. She kept a roof over my head, but I was happy to get out on my own," she answered.

"Well, if it were a handicap, you could have fooled me. You're about as capable as any woman or man I know with perfect vision."

"I knew there was something I liked about you." She smiled.

"I should probably get going. Can I set your computer someplace for you?"

"Oh, yeah. The dining room table is fine."

Mason stepped through her doorway and moved to set it down.

When he returned to the front door, he watched her hang up her coat and set her keys on the small table beside the stairs. He could already see her routine, everything had its place so that it didn't get in her way and presumably would be easy for her to find later on. He noticed she'd set her cane in the closet with her coat and he assumed she was familiar enough with her surroundings so that it wasn't needed here anymore than it was required in the diner.

When she turned back to the doorway, he reached his hand out to take hers once again and rubbed his thumb over her knuckles.

"I'm going to head out. Will I see you at the diner in the morning?"

"If you come back into the kitchen, you will." She smiled.

"Is that an invitation?" he asked.

"Very astute of you, Mr. Cole." She laughed.

"Well then, I'll see you in the morning," Mason said as he started to turn for the door. He turned back before he let go of her hand and let his lips lightly brush over her knuckles. "Sleep well," he said as he walked out into the frigid air.

He stood on the steps and waited until he heard the lock engage, and then he jogged back in the direction of the diner towards his house. Not even the cold could wipe the smile from his face. When he got home, he took a hot shower and climbed into his bed for the first time in what seemed like ages, having slept on his couch more often than not. He sent Devon a text telling him to pick him up at the diner at seven-thirty instead of his place, and then he closed his eyes and slept until his alarm went off at six the following morning.

Chapter 3

Mason walked into the diner at twenty minutes to seven.

"Molly?" he asked the young girl at the counter.

"Hi. You must be Mason. Colleen and Judy weren't kidding when they said you were hot," Molly said.

Mason just laughed and pointed towards the back.

"Oh, yeah. Go on back," the young waitress said as a deep blush painted her cheeks. "I'll pack up your order and brew the coffee in a few minutes so it's nice and hot."

"Thanks, Molly."

Mason walked back into the kitchen and said, "Good morning."

"Good morning to you!" she said as she washed the flour from her hands.

A chime sounded and an electronic voice indicated that it was six forty-five.

"You're early. How about a cup of coffee? Or are you in a hurry this morning?" she asked.

"Nope. My brother is picking me up here at seven-thirty."

"Plenty of time, then," she stated as she reached out for his hand. Mason stepped forward and caught her hand in his as she led him back out to a table in the corner.

Molly came out a minute later and set two cups of coffee and a basket with warm blueberry and peach-almond muffins on the table.

"How is it that I've been coming here for months and I never discovered how incredible these smell?" Mason stated as the aroma wafted from the basket.

"Well, you usually come in late at night. So you go for something more substantial or you stick with the coffee. They have to be hot out of the oven to get the full appreciation," she said as she pulled the napkin open that was keeping the muffins warm.

They each pulled out a muffin, and Mason watched as Dakota closed her eyes and let the sweet scent of almonds and peaches permeate her senses. He closed his eyes and tried to experience the muffin as she did. The smell seemed so much more potent as he breathed it in. When he opened his eyes, he took a minute just to look at Dakota before he broke open the muffin. Her hair was a rich brown that almost looked like melted dark chocolate when the light hit it just right. It hung loose around her shoulders in a shiny curtain that nearly begged to be touched and her skin was so pale that it almost had a translucent quality to it. Her lashes were still touching her cheeks when a soft smile began to form on her lips.

"You're staring," she stated.

"Guilty as charged," he said as a flush colored his cheeks once again.

He thought it was a shame she couldn't enjoy his embarrassment. Mason laughed a little as he lifted her hand to his cheek so that she could feel the heat rise.

"It can't be helped. You are really stunning when you experience something that you clearly enjoy. It makes me want to experience the world the way that you do," he said as he let his thumb move in soft circles over the back of her hand, which rested against his cheek.

"Do you always blush like that? I would have guessed you were more of a ladies' man." Dakota said as she let her fingers slide across the rough stubble on his cheek.

"Honestly, no. My brother would tell you that I never get embarrassed. So this is all new to me," he whispered.

"Hmmm. Will I get to meet him today?" she asked.

"Maybe. I'm pretty sure I won't be able to keep him away once he realizes I come here for more than just the coffee," Mason said with a laugh.

"Oh? And what do you come for?"

"Well, I used to come for the coffee, true but, I was intrigued by the pretty girl who always sat across the aisle. Since I met her, I have so many more reasons to keep coming back. Apart from your baking skills, I just really like you," Mason told her as he let his fingers softly graze her cheek, too.

The bell chimed above the door, but neither of them even registered the new arrival.

"I knew there was a reason you picked this diner!" Devon said as he walked towards their table. "So, little brother, care to introduce me to your friend?" The smile on his face was so bright it was nearly audible.

Dakota held her hand out towards Devon and said, "I'm Dakota, and you must be Devon."

Devon grasped her hand and said, "The one and only, but feel free to call me 'Dev.' Everyone else does. I guess my brother kept you a secret because he was afraid my boyish good looks would be too much for you to resist."

Dakota laughed out loud before she said, "I don't know if that would have worked to your advantage considering looks aren't really my thing."

"You do realize you're the first woman to sit across from this mug and not spout off about how beautiful he is? Have I met the first woman immune to the 'Mason Effect'?" Devon questioned as he watched her take a sip of her coffee.

"Oh, she's not immune," Molly said as she set a cup of coffee in front of Devon.

"Nope, I'm blind, but I'm definitely not immune," Dakota added. Devon laughed until something about her words clicked.

"Oh shit, you're serious. She's serious?" Devon asked.

"Of course I am. I've been blind since I was four. I just happen to be pretty adept at living in a sighted world." She smiled. "Just because I'm blind doesn't mean I don't 'see' the world around me."

"I guess not," Devon said as he looked at his brother, who was smiling at Dakota.

"For instance, I can tell you're shorter than your brother, but you aren't exactly the beast to his beauty are you?" She smiled.

"How do you know I'm shorter?" Devon asked as he looked at his brother, who sat watching the two as he drank his coffee and enjoyed a muffin.

"It took you ten steps to get to the table from the front door. It only takes Mason seven. You balked at the comment about being shorter, so it's come up before, but people don't usually accuse you of being unattractive based on the fact that you didn't show even an ounce of insecurity over your looks. Plus, I know you're attractive because of the way Molly was when she came over. Usually she talks a mile a minute with male customers. And I know it's not your brother that had her tongue-tied because she was bending his ear when he came in earlier. So, it has to be you," Dakota explained.

"Wow. Pretty and observant," Devon said as he helped himself to the muffins. "Oh. My. God. We're coming here for breakfast every day!"

"Amazing, right?" Mason asked. "Wait until you try the cinnamon rolls that Dakota made for us to take to the station."

"If it's anything like this, you won't hear me complaining!" Devon answered around a mouthful of blueberry muffin.

"Be thankful that you can't see what a Neanderthal my big brother is," Mason offered by way of apology.

Dakota laughed and said, "Speaking of orders, what time is it?"

"It's almost seven thirty. I guess we should get going," Mason said. "Dev, why don't you go grab my order from Molly?"

"Okay, Mase. I can take a hint; I'll leave you two alone. It was really nice to meet you, Dakota," he said as he patted Mason quite firmly on the back.

"You as well, Dev," she responded with a smile.

"Will you be here tonight?" Mason asked as he stood up.

"Of course. I'll go home in an hour or so, and then come back after dinner to prep for tomorrow," she said.

"Then I'll stop by tonight," he whispered as he gently let his hand rest on her shoulder.

"I'll be here."

"Come on, Casanova. We have to get these to the station before I open the box or there won't be anything left for Mel and Piper," Devon said as he headed out the door.

Mason laughed as he followed and said, "I'll see you later."

"So, you've been holding out on me. I knew there had to be something. You've lost that surly edge we've come to associate with you. This is a good thing, and she seems like a really nice girl."

"She is very nice. And in a few minutes, you will be appreciating her skills in the kitchen even more. If you thought the muffins were amazing, the cinnamon rolls are even better."

"Write it down, because this is the first time I'm wishing we could leave food in my car," Devon said. "They smell outstanding. I think I might have to Bogart your spot, dude."

"We'll talk about it," Mason told him as they pulled into the station's parking lot.

Mason grabbed the box from the back seat as Devon grabbed the coffee and headed into their office where Mel and Piper were waiting.

"I'd complain that you're late, but then I probably wouldn't get whatever is in the box. Since it smells so good, I think I'll keep my complaints to myself," Piper said.

"Good move, buddy. You do not want to miss out on these," Devon said as he opened the box.

The four of them descended on the box and the aroma started to filter out into the hallway. Within seconds, others were stopping in with the hopes of sampling whatever was wafting into the other offices.

Mason smiled as he watched everyone enjoy Dakota's cinnamon rolls and made sure everyone knew where they came from. He was certain Dakota would have half of the police force coming in on a regular basis. He just hoped they didn't decide to stop in when he was around, because he selfishly wanted Dakota all to himself.

After everyone had filtered out of the serial crimes bullpen, Mason got right down to business.

"So what do we know today that we didn't know yesterday?" he asked Melinda.

"Well, surprisingly little. Aside from obvious similarities in the wounds and the ID, there is nothing that is apparent in terms of linking Julianne to Jill. Julianne was adopted, but the records are sealed. I'm working on getting them un-sealed. Jill's parents died when she was in college, right?"

"I'm pretty sure her dad died when she was little. She didn't really talk much about it. I think her mom is still alive or at least that's the impression I got. But based on what I know, she might as well have been dead. They didn't speak at all that I was aware

Kristi Loucks

of. Do we have anything to go on yet?" Mason asked as he rubbed his palm over his face.

"I'm sorry, Mase. It looks like we're in neutral until the adoption records are unsealed or...." the young analyst answered.

They all looked at one another, but didn't want to voice the next thought: Or, until someone else dies at the hands of the killer.

After eight hours of pouring over the evidence from the two cases and the surveillance videos from the Howard's building, they still had more questions than answers. They knew it would take time to get the adoption records unsealed, so for the time being there was nothing for them to do but wait.

At half past nine, Mason decided to call it a night. His team had left several hours earlier with the hopes that fresh eyes and a new day would shed light on some piece of evidence they had yet to uncover, but they all knew that was unlikely.

Instead of heading home as he normally would, Mason found himself walking in the direction of the diner. The frigid temperature went unnoticed as he allowed his mind to pick apart the case details once again.

It was a little before ten when he finally arrived at the diner. The chime over the door alerted Judy of his arrival. She looked up and smiled as she pulled two coffee cups from the shelf behind her. Mason met her at the counter and asked, "Can I take it in the back? I'll bring one for Dakota, too."

"Sure, sweetheart. I'm sure she'd love the interruption," Judy said as she smiled at him.

Mason walked into the kitchen and heard the radio playing in the background. He stood in the doorway and watched as Dakota moved to the music. He loved that she lived her life in such an un-choreographed fashion. Most of the women he dealt with calculated their every move, which was why he'd avoided relationships for most of his adult life. Up until now, Jill had been the only exception.

He liked that he saw the unedited version of the woman standing before him. She was fascinating and real. She was quickly becoming important to him and he was charmed by her easy appreciation of the world around her. Despite what she physically could not see, the world was a bright and open place in her eyes, a much-needed counterbalance to the life he saw every day.

"I can tell you're standing there, Mase," she said as she continued to move to the music.

"Was it the coffee that tipped you off?" he asked, wondering how she'd known.

"No. The coffee could have been Judy, but the last time I checked, she doesn't smell like Gauthier."

"True enough. It's kind of interesting, the things you pick up on considering I haven't put anything on since six this morning. I kind of like it," he said as he pushed off the wall and walked over to set the coffee cups down on the counter behind where she stood. "What are you working on here?"

"It's our challah. We use it for our French toast. Here, wash your hands and I'll show you how to braid it," she said.

Mason stepped over to the sink and washed his hands before he returned to her side. She started by showing him how to lay out the ropes of dough with only the top ends touching, then she took his hands in hers as he stood behind her and guided his movements to create the braid. He smiled as he noticed how small she felt standing in front of him. The top of her head barely reached the middle of his chest and her tiny hands barely covered his.

The task was one he'd never have thought himself capable of, but he was learning there were a lot of things he could see himself doing with this woman. She made him want to see the world like she did, instead of the dark place it had become to him.

After the challah was finished, he watched as she braided the rest of the loaves effortlessly. When she had wrapped them to rest in the cooler overnight, Mason helped her clean up the kitchen before they refilled their coffee and headed to the table they'd basically claimed as their own out front.

"So how was your day today?" she asked.

"Long. I came here straight from work," he answered.

"Wow. It's well after ten, isn't it? That is a long day," she said. She was quiet as she considered her next thought. "I understand if you can't answer, but do you have a case?"

"We always have cases; it's just that we have a case right now that we've been working for a long time. It's the case that made me take this job in the first place, but it's been cold for almost a year."

"And it's not anymore?" she wondered aloud.

"No, unfortunately, it's not," he answered with a hint of sadness.

"Well, I'm here if you need someone to talk to. About the case, or anything else," she offered.

He touched her hand as he said, "Thanks. I appreciate that." As soon as the words left his mouth, his phone started to ring. Mason pulled it from his pocket, looking at the caller ID. "What is it Dev?" he answered.

"I hate to ruin your time with Dakota, but I'm on my way to you. We've got another body."

"Shit. Is it our guy?" Mason asked.

"Looks like."

"Meet me six blocks west of the diner. I'm going to walk Dakota home. I'll wait out front," he said as she got up and went behind the counter to grab her things.

"Okay, Mase, see you in a few," Devon said as he disconnected the call.

Mason moved towards the back and grabbed her computer bag from her, setting it aside to help her get her coat on.

"Goodnight, Judy," they both said as they headed towards the door.

Mason slung her bag over his shoulder as she reached for his hand.

"You don't have to walk me home. I've managed this long," she said as she smiled.

"Call me old-fashioned, but I like walking you home. And I get to spend a few more minutes with you. Win, win," he said as she squeezed her hand.

Mason opened the door and the pair stepped out onto the sidewalk and into the unforgiving Chicago winter. When he felt Dakota shudder just a bit, he took the opening to put his arm around her shoulder and pull her closer to his side. This time the cane stayed in the bag while she relied on him to keep her from

32

any unexpected obstacles, but just as he'd thought, she managed to walk most of the way home without any guidance from him.

"Cold?" he asked.

"Who wouldn't be?" she stated. "So, I take it something happened with your case?"

"It seems so. We won't know for sure until we get there," he answered.

She nodded silently, knowing that she wouldn't get any additional information.

"Will you be in early tomorrow? Can I come by and grab a cup of coffee with you before I go in to work?" he asked.

"I practically live there, and of course I would be happy for a distraction. Especially if that distraction is you," she whispered as she leaned into his body to absorb his warmth.

"Then, I would be more than happy to distract you. Maybe around seven?" he asked.

"That sounds good to me."

"Here we are," he said as he turned them towards her front steps. "Want me to put your computer on the table?"

"Sure. I need to put the trash out. I'll be right back," she said as she walked into the kitchen.

Before she made it out the back door with the trash, she felt Mason's hand on hers as he took the bag. "Is the bin in the alley?"

"Yes." She laughed. "Thank you."

He came back in and locked the back door before he walked back over to her. "It's no problem. I guess you've been taking care of yourself for a long time now?" he asked.

"Yes. I've been living on my own about nine years give or take, but I'll admit it's nice to have someone take my trash out," she said with a smile.

"I bet. Well, I should get out front before Dev wakes up the neighborhood. He should be here any minute."

She followed him to the door and he turned back and said, "Goodnight, Dakota. I'll see you in the morning."

When he didn't turn away immediately, she smiled and then she felt his breath caress her cheek softly before his lips brushed over her right temple.

"Sleep well," he whispered, and then he was gone.

Dakota heard him close the door and wait for her to engage the lock. As she did, she whispered, "Goodnight," and let her hand rest against her skin, still tingling from his kiss.

She managed to get through her nightly routine quickly and fell asleep with thoughts of Mason Cole and the way he'd quickly become an important part of her life. Somehow, she'd known that first night they'd spoken that he wouldn't remain a stranger for long.

Chapter 4

"So, you've been to her house. Interesting," Devon stated as Mason got into the car.

"I realize that you are incredibly interested in my personal life, but I think now would be a better time to talk about the new development in the case," Mason grumbled.

"Fine, but don't think for a second that we won't get back to this new development," Devon said before he rolled into the case details.

"We're not sure if this is our guy. If it is, then he is changing up his MO and expanding to killing men, too. The victim is in his early twenties. He's pre-med at Northwestern. Name is Jonathon Beauford. Campus Security was first on the scene and called it in. The responding officer recognized the 'staging' apparently, and called it in to Serial Crimes."

"So he's going after guys now? I don't understand. There doesn't seem to be a discernible pattern here. He's all over the map with men, women, different ages, different physical attributes, and careers. How is he choosing his victims? There has to be something that ties them all together."

"The parents are on their way. They called local PD after they didn't hear from him when they expected. Desk gave them the standard missing 24 hours and college students breaking away from their parents' spiel, so they called the school and campus security called it in an hour ago. So, don't be anticipating a warm reception. Dr. Hovey arrived a few minutes ago; she should be able to give us more when we get there."

"Kade and Torello are on their way?" Mason asked.

"Should be there a few minutes behind us. It took me a couple of tries to get through to Melinda. Apparently, you aren't the only one I need to question about their personal life. And Piper was at a movie with his flavor of the day. No sense questioning him; we all know she won't be around in a few days," Devon joked.

"Yeah. I keep thinking one of these days, some girl is going to turn his life upside down, and he'll quit being such a dog. I mean, I know he isn't leading these girls on, but seriously, how much fun can a different girl every night really be?"

"Oh come on. You weren't too different back in the day," Devon said as he poked his brother in the side.

"No, I guess not. But, that wore off once I figured out getting laid wouldn't fill the void losing Mom and Dad left. I mean I wasn't a monk or anything, but I started to be a little more careful about the women I let into my bed."

"Yeah, but ever since Jill you've been a lot more than careful. So much so that you didn't even see the women throwing themselves at you. I'm glad that you noticed Dakota though. I like her," Devon said as they pulled up outside the apartment complex just on the edge of campus.

"She didn't exactly throw herself at me, but I like her, too. She fascinates me," Mason added.

Devon smiled at his brother's candid remark as they made their way to the lobby. "She didn't need to throw herself at you."

"No, she sure didn't. I noticed her the first time I saw her, but I wasn't really doing a lot of talking back then."

As they walked into the lobby, Mason noticed the campus security guard coming their way. "Hello, Roger," he said as he read his nametag. "I'm Lt. Commander Mason Cole and this is Detective Devon Cole. We're with Serial Crimes. I take it you are campus security. Can you walk me through the last hour or so?"

"I was sitting in my office when Mrs. Beauford called for the third time. She seemed pretty hysterical, so I told her I'd check on her boy as soon as my shift ended. That was two hours later. Oh, God! If I'd have checked sooner, maybe I could have helped that poor boy," the older gentleman said as he broke down.

"Sir, I'm so sorry. I know this has to be difficult. But based on what we already know, I don't think that two hours would have helped him. You did everything you could for him," Devon said as he laid a hand on his shoulder.

"I thought I'd find him in bed with a cold or perhaps a young lady or even a monster hangover. That's usually why kids don't call their parents when they get out on their own. I just wasn't prepared to find him..." Roger dropped his head in his hands as the words just stopped coming.

"It's okay sir. Officer Jackson is going to take you down to the station and get a statement. The fact that you came all the way out here after your shift will be a comfort to the Beaufords," Mason told the man as Officer Jackson ushered him out to his squad car.

Mason turned and headed for the stairs, taking them two at a time with Devon right behind him. The hallway was alive with dozens of officers questioning the other residents about what they may have seen or heard. And Mason was almost certain they'd seen and heard nothing. Melinda and Piper had arrived as they made their way down the hallway to the victim's apartment.

They entered the apartment and instantly smelled the acrid tang of copper. Blood dripped in fat droplets from the ceiling, indicating that his latest victim's heart had been pumping at the time the wounds were inflicted.

Mason closed his eyes as he prepared himself to enter the room fully. When he opened them, he moved to the left where he saw Dr. Hovey crouched over the body of the young victim. His eyes had been taped open; his hands were extended out to the side and duct taped to the metal slats of his headboard.

The carotid artery was gaping open with a solid stream of dried blood coating his skin and leaving the unmistakable spray pattern on the ceiling and walls. His mouth was duct taped to silence his screams and he had a tourniquet on his left arm that prevented him from bleeding out as the killer warmed up with his brachial and radial arteries. Dried blood had dripped from his nose, covering the tape that kept him silent, and the sheets beneath him were saturated with blood and urine. Undoubtedly, this poor young man had spent the last hours of his life in an unimaginable state of terror.

"Looks like the handiwork of your guy," Dr. Hovey stated. "No hesitation marks. Each incision is methodical and precise."

"Yeah. He's enjoying this, too. He wants them to watch, to see the life drain from their bodies. He wants to be the last thing they see," Mason said as he glanced around the room.

"Anyone find any roses?" Devon asked as he looked for the signature, too.

"No, not yet," Melinda said as she walked into the kitchen. "But there's an envelope on the refrigerator with your name on it, Mase." She walked over and placed the envelope in his gloved hand.

"Sorry to interrupt, it appears there may be something lodged in his throat," Dr. Hovey said.

The team turned back towards the victim as Dr. Hovey carefully pulled tape from his mouth before placing it in a plastic evidence bag. His jaw was clamped shut, but they could clearly see a protrusion surrounding his throat. Piper moved to the side and helped Dr. Hovey pry the victim's mouth open.

"Oh, God," Melinda said when she saw what had been shoved down the victim's throat; a single white rose that had an ominous pinkish hue undoubtedly from the victim's own blood.

Dr. Hovey took out a pair of forceps and grabbed the rose, trying to keep it intact. Mason's stomach turned when the rose didn't pop out in one pull; it became apparent that the stem had been forced all the way down his throat. Dr. Hovey had just placed the rose in a bag as her assistant came in pushing a gurney to transport the body to the morgue.

"That is just sick. What could this kid have done to deserve that?" Devon asked as he walked away.

Mason followed, still carrying the envelope and the rose in his hand as they moved into the kitchen so that Dr. Hovey could transport the body and get started on the autopsy.

When everyone had a moment to digest what had transpired, Mason pulled his knife out and slid it under the envelope's flap. He turned it over, letting the contents spill onto the countertop and he began to sift through it.

On top, there was a smaller envelope. The outside was free of any writing, so Mason pulled the card from within. This time, there was only a single bloody fingerprint and the signature.

ROSE RED REAPER

"Somehow, I doubt that he's stupid enough to give us a fingerprint and sign his name to it," Devon said.

"Yeah. I doubt it, but if I had to guess, it will tie back to Julianne Howard. He likes to confirm his kills," Mason said.

Piper quickly took a photo of the print with his phone and ran it through a print database. There was a ping alerting a match almost instantly, and the match was in fact Julianne Howard.

Mason went back to the envelope and found several photographs of Julianne Howard and another of an unidentified woman that appeared to be at a train station, perhaps somewhere on the North Shore.

"Melinda, can we start a search and see if we can figure out where this is. Maybe this is a clue to his next victim? Let's see if we can't get a step ahead," he said as he placed the pictures back in the envelope.

"Got it. Piper, are you heading back to the station, or should I get a lift from one of the uniforms?" she asked.

"Mase, do you need me to stick around?" he asked.

"No. If you're done cataloging evidence and getting photos, you're good to go."

"We'll see you in an hour or so. The family is going straight to the station, so keep a look out for them. I want our team to handle them since they already feel that the police dropped the ball in checking on their son," Devon said as they headed for the door.

Devon and Mason made their way out into the hallway and talked to the officers who had canvassed the building. There had been no signs of forced entry and as expected, none of the other residents had seen or heard anything unusual.

When the landlord arrived, he told them that the surveillance cameras were dummies, so that wouldn't help them at all. Since the apartment complex wasn't on campus, there were no cameras outside either. The closest they got was the traffic light at Sheridan and Lincoln, which was half a block from the building. It was a busy intersection, but it was also easily avoidable. Besides, without knowing exactly who or what they were looking for it wouldn't tell them much of anything unless the killer happened to be wearing a neon sign that said, "ROSE RED REAPER."

They were going to need more information before they'd be able to garner any new information from the traffic camera, provided he'd even used that particular intersection.

After several hours of fact checking, Mason and Devon decided to head back to their offices and check in with Piper and Melinda.

"Have the parents arrived yet?" Mason asked the desk clerk.

"Yes, sir, someone just escorted them to your office, just as Detective Torello instructed," the clerk said.

"Thanks. Could you call up and let Torello know we're on our way?"

"No problem," he answered as he picked up the phone and did as he was asked.

Melinda was just returning with bottles of water for the Beaufords when Devon and Mason arrived. "How do they seem?" he asked.

"About as you would expect. They just came from giving an ID on their son, so they're definitely devastated, confused, and angry," she told him.

"I know the feeling. You two should keep looking at the evidence. Dev and I will go see what we can find out from the Beaufords."

As they entered the room, Mason handed Mr. and Mrs. Beauford a bottle of water before introducing himself. "Mr. and Mrs. Beauford, I am Lt. Commander Mason Cole and this is Detective Devon Cole. Your son's case has been handed over to our unit. I am so sorry for your loss. I know how difficult it must be," Mason said.

"Pardon me, son, but how could you have any idea what we are going through?" a distraught Mr. Beauford asked.

Mason pulled a picture from his wallet and slid it across the table in front of the Beaufords. It was the last picture he'd taken with Jill on Navy Pier a few weeks before she died. "Sir, I came to this unit because someone that I cared for was stolen from me, too. I wish I could bring all of the people back that have been lost at the hands of a killer, but bringing the people responsible to justice is the best I can offer."

Mr. Beauford nodded as he passed the picture back across the table. The older man rubbed his eyes as he whispered, "I'm sorry. I just never thought I'd be sitting here listening to someone tell me my son is gone."

"I know, sir. You have nothing to be sorry about. I understand," Mason said, putting the picture back in his wallet.

"I'll try to keep this short, but we do have a few questions, if you don't mind," Devon said.

Once again, the Beaufords nodded. Mrs. Beauford was obviously in a state of shock over the traumatic events that had occurred in the last several hours as she sobbed softly against her husband's shoulder.

"Can you tell us about your son? Did he tell you anything recently that seemed odd?"

"Our son was a good kid. He got excellent grades and worked hard. He had two jobs, one at a bar just off campus a few nights a week and the sub shop near his apartment a couple of afternoons a week. As far as we knew, everything was normal," Mr. Beauford stated.

"No, that's not entirely true, Gene," Mrs. Beauford interrupted. "Someone had contacted Jon about a month ago about a genealogy project from the science department. He'd assumed it was a student, but the man didn't actually say that. He asked a bunch of questions regarding our family, and Jon thought it was strange since he was adopted. He knows nothing of his biological family, so he declined to participate. He said the man got angry and started ranting about privilege and opportunities, so Jon hung up. He never heard from the man again."

"How old was Jon when you adopted him?" Mason asked.

"About four."

"Was he adopted through an agency?" Mason continued.

"Yes. Brentwood, I believe, was the name of the agency. They are in Northern Wisconsin where we live."

"Do you know anything about where he came from?"

"No. It was a closed adoption, but he suffered from horrific nightmares for a few years after we adopted him. Oh, God, I know something horrible happened before he came to us, but we never knew much about his life before. Do you think that has anything to do with what happened?" Mrs. Beauford replied as tears continued to stream down her face.

41

"We're not certain of anything just yet, but we have to take everything into account," Devon told the woman.

"Do you recall what the nightmares were about?" Mason asked.

"Roses. That was all he ever said. He was so little, he didn't talk much then, and by the time he started talking more, he wasn't suffering the nightmares as often," Mrs. Beauford answered as her tears finally turned into an uncontrollable sob, making it obvious that this was as far as they'd get tonight.

Mason and Devon looked at one another, as that one word became a clue that could blow this case wide open. If only they could figure out how it fit in with the rest of the victims.

"I'm sorry. I know this must be tough. We'd like for you to stay in town for the next few days while we investigate in case anything more comes up. We already booked a room for you at the Marriott a few miles down from here, so we can have someone take you there now."

After the Beaufords were escorted to their hotel, Mason and Devon headed into the other room to check in with Piper and Melinda.

"What have you come up with?" Mason said as he walked into the bullpen.

Melinda quickly pushed her chair back, walked over to the computer table, and pushed the photos to the monitors on the wall. "This is the photo of the woman at the train station. Based on the trim work on the building, it looks like the East Lake Forest train station. No ID on the woman yet, as it turns out this picture is at least fifteen years old," she said.

"Really? How can you pinpoint that?" Devon asked.

"I pulled the plates on the car in the background, the BMW with the L4 X3M9 plate. It was totaled in a head-on collision in 1997; I have the accident report right here. So this picture had to be taken before that," Piper said.

"They could have gotten a new car with the same plates though," Mason said.

"Nope. Driver was Walter Hartrey. His wife, Amber, was in the passenger seat. Had a couple of kids, but they weren't in the car. Driver of the other car was Angela Forrester; she survived with minor lacerations from the air bags and a broken arm. No charges were filed, evidently the traffic light wasn't functioning properly," Piper clarified.

"So, do you think the clue is the woman, the people who died in that crash, or both?" Mason wondered out loud.

"The woman in the photo is deceased. She died of cancer shortly after the photo was taken. Her name was Susan Waters. So, it doesn't seem likely that she is the clue, but we'll look into it further just in case," Piper said.

"Wait, do you think the clue could be the crash itself?" Melinda asked.

"I wouldn't rule it out. At the moment, we don't KNOW anything for sure. Until we do, we should assume everything is a clue. The Beaufords said Jonathon was adopted and that he was plagued by nightmares when he first came to them. Nightmares about roses. That has to be important; I just don't know how it fits yet. But, it's all we have. Right now, we know that two of the victims were adopted, but there is no direct link in terms of dates, locations, or agencies for any of the victims. What we don't know is how Jill fits in, because as far as I know she was never in the system. There has to be something we are missing. Adoption has to be the common ground," Mason said.

"Okay, then we'll start looking deeper at adoption records. And I'll look into the owner of the car and the accident itself, as if that were perhaps our primary crime scene. If that is what started him on this path, I guess it sort of is the primary by default," Piper added.

"All right, go home and get some sleep. You can look further into Susan Waters' history tomorrow. You're going to have to wait until a more reasonable hour anyway, since I don't think anyone will be too forthcoming at four in the morning. I'll send a request to unseal the adoption records. Hopefully that will give us more to go on. Dev, call over to the lab; Andy and Robin can go through the video from the traffic cam as well as run screens when Dr. Hovey finishes the autopsy. Tomorrow we'll get back at it with fresh eyes. We'll meet back here, say, around ten," Mason ordered. "Coffee and muffins are on me."

Everyone smiled, knowing that there was more to that story, but fortunately, they were all too exhausted to break into interrogation mode.

"Come on, little brother. I'll take you home. I'm crashing in your guest room tonight," Devon said.

"Okay, but then you're buying coffee and muffins tomorrow," he said with a laugh.

"As long as I'm buying them from your girl at the diner, that's fine by me. Maybe she'll tell me what's going on with the two of you." He smirked.

"Whatever, I'm driving," Mason said as he got to the car.

They rode in silence to the house and made their way to their own beds before passing out from exhaustion. The day had taken a heavy toll on all of them.

Chapter 5

Mason's alarm went off at six. He rolled over to grab his phone and dialed.

"Shelton's Diner, this is Molly. How can I help you this morning?" Molly answered.

"Good morning, Molly. This is Mason Cole. We met yesterday."

"I remember. What can I do for you?" she asked.

"Can I order two dozen muffins and two of the coffee setups like we had yesterday? I'll pick it up around 9:30-ish. Does that work?"

"Sure thing. Anything else?"

"Is Dakota around?" he asked.

"Sure. Want me to get her for you?"

"Please, if she's not too busy." He listened to the daily specials while he was on hold until Dakota picked up.

"Hi, Mason. Are you coming in?" she asked.

"Yeah. Devon and I will be in around nine. It was a really late night. I didn't want you to worry when I didn't show up at seven, though."

"I would have worried, so thanks for letting me know," she said. "Are you okay?"

"Better now. I woke up and realized I didn't have your phone number, so I'm glad that you were at the diner."

"Well, you can always call here. If I'm not around, they can find me," she said.

Mason could hear the timer blaring in the background, so he said, "Well, I'll let you go. I know you have a lot to get done. I'll see you in a few hours, okay?"

"All right. Try to go back to sleep. Oh, and Mase?"

"Yeah?" he said around a yawn.

"Sleep well," she whispered.

"I will," he said. He quickly fell back to sleep with a smile on his face.

A few hours later, his cell phone chirped with a new text message from a number he didn't recognize.

Your order will be ready in half an hour. We'll brew the coffee whenever you get here. D

It chirped again.

Now you have my number :)

Mason walked into the bathroom and turned on the shower, the smile never leaving his face. As the water warmed up, he picked up his phone and added her number to his contacts before calling her.

Dakota picked up on the first ring.

"Good morning. Now that I have your number, I wanted to call and ask a very important question."

"What's that, Mase?" He could hear the smile in her voice.

"Can I take you to dinner sometime?"

"I think I could be persuaded to go to dinner with you," she answered.

"Can someone cover for you at the diner?"

"Judy's daughter Colleen can cover the prep. What did you have in mind?"

"That I can't tell you. I need to make a few calls. Would Friday work?" Mason asked, hoping that the current case wouldn't ruin his plans.

"I'll call Colleen right now," she told him.

"Okay. Then it's a date," he said as his smile grew.

"See you in a bit," she said before she hung up the phone.

Mason quickly undressed and stepped under the hot spray, mulling over all the things they could do on their date. Once he was dressed and ready to go, he walked down the hall and banged on the door to the guest room before shouting, "Dev, get up. I'm going to head over to the diner. Come down when you're ready. Don't forget, you're buying today!"

He heard Devon groan as he got out of bed and turned on the shower, indicating it was safe for him to head out without taking extreme measures to wake up his brother

The sun was out as Mason walked to the diner and he was feeling much more rested than he'd expected after the night they'd had. When he walked into the diner, Molly greeted him

46

and waved him back to where Dakota was working. She handed him a cup of coffee on his way by.

"Thanks, Molly. How are you this morning?" he asked.

"I'm good. You look like a happy camper this morning. Dakota is wearing the same goofy smile as you are. Is it safe to assume you're to blame?" She smiled.

"I can't speak for her, but she is certainly to blame for my good mood," he said as he made his way back to the kitchen.

When he walked into the kitchen, he found Dakota listening to the radio as she wiped down the counters. He glanced around, deciding that she must have finished with her prep for later that evening and she was getting ready to head home for the afternoon.

"Can I help you clean up? I'll even buy you a cup of coffee," he said as he walked over to her.

"Good morning," she said as she turned towards him and held out her hand.

Mason stepped forward and grasped the hand she'd extended, placing it on his shoulder as he pulled her a little closer. "So, about this date..." he started.

"Yes, about that."

"What kind of food do you like?" he asked as he swayed to the music with her in his arms.

"Spicy. Thai or maybe Mexican?" she told him.

"Mmmm. I like spicy food and a woman who knows what she wants. Now that we've got that taken care of, do you like to dance?" he asked.

"I love to, as long as it's not too crowded," she whispered as she let her hand slide up to his neck from where he'd placed it on his shoulder.

"I can work with that," he answered. "Red or white?"

"Beer, but not light beer please," she answered with a laugh. "Are you going to tell me anything?"

"You are definitely my kind of woman. Dress comfortably and warm. I know the perfect place and it's not far."

"That's all I get? It's a good thing I trust you."

"Oh no. You should never trust this one," Devon said as he came around the corner.

"Dev," Mason said with a hint of irritation.

"Mase. Dakota. What are you doing back here?" he asked as he gave them the once over, taking note of their close proximity.

"Waiting on you, lazy bones," Dakota said without missing a beat as she breezed by the laughing intrusion on her otherwise perfect morning. Mason liked seeing her in her element; she moved effortlessly in familiar surroundings and he loved her confidence.

"I like her," Devon said as he walked out to join her.

"Me, too," Mason said to no one as he followed.

As he made it out to the table, Molly came over with 3 cups of coffee and a basket of warm muffins.

Mason slid into the booth beside Dakota and put her coffee cup in front of her left hand. "Here you go," he said as he lightly touched her fingers to the handle.

"Thanks."

Devon eyed the two of them carefully with a smile on his face. It was easily the most relaxed he'd seen his brother and that was something, considering everything that was happening outside of the diner lately. The three of them talked for a few minutes until their order was all packed up and the coffee was ready.

"Did you just throw this whole thing together now?" Devon asked as Molly brought over the two containers of coffee and two boxes of muffins.

"No. Mason placed the order this morning when he called to say he'd be late," Dakota answered.

"Really. He called, did he?" Devon asked as he made a face at his brother.

"Molly, he's paying today," Mason said, which promptly shut Devon up, at least for a few minutes anyway.

Dakota just laughed at the pair of them. "You two are something else."

Devon walked over to the counter to pay for their order.

"Can I walk you home tonight?" Mason asked.

"I'll be here. If you're available, then I'd love for you to walk me home." She laughed.

Mason kissed her cheek and said goodbye before jogging out to the car after his brother.

"So...." Devon said.

"So…what?" Mason answered in a similar tone.

"A little slow dancing in the kitchen? She looks good on you. I mean, check that smile you can barely contain, little brother."

"I asked her out on a date."

"Well. This is new. Where are you taking her?"

"I didn't tell her, so I'm sure as hell not telling you!" Mason said as he smiled at his brother. There was a brief silence and Mason could see his brother mulling over something more serious.

"Does she know about Jill?" Devon asked quietly as the air was seemingly sucked from the confines of the car.

"Why would you go and ruin it by saying that? Geez, Dev! She knows something happened and that it prompted my career change, but that's not the kind of thing you say over coffee!"

"There will never be a good time."

"Sure, I'll just say 'let me get that door for you and by the way, the killer we're after…I think he's the same guy that murdered my girlfriend, Jill about a year ago. Let's go get some Thai food?' I bet that would go over really well!"

"Well, now that you put it that way," Devon said with a shrug.

"Look, I really like her. The last thing I want to do is scare her off before I even get around to kissing her."

"Whoa, back that up a bit. You haven't even kissed her yet?"

"No. Well, not a real kiss. Yet."

"Pardon me for being dense, but is there a fake kind of kiss?" Devon asked.

"Kissing her on the cheek or hand isn't even close to the same thing," Mason said as he looked at his brother.

"Huh. I never would have taken you for the patient type."

"Oh, I'm not. And it's not getting any easier," Mason confided as they pulled up in front of the precinct.

Devon handed the boxes to Mason as he got out of the car and grabbed the coffee as he followed him up to their offices.

"You know, I might need to meet this woman, because I think I love her," Melinda said.

"Me, too," Piper added.

"Melinda, I'm sure she'd love to meet you," Mason said as he glared at Piper.

49

"Okay, man, I see how it is. Consider the territory marked, big guy."

Devon just laughed as he moved over to the computer to look at the email from the lab that Mason had pulled up.

Good morning, Mason,

We have gone through the evidence from last night's case and found very little in terms of identifying the killer, but we did learn a little more about some of the evidence that could help narrow the search perhaps. Stop by when you get a chance.

Andy

Before Devon was even finished reading, Mason already had his coat on and was halfway out the door.

"So, I guess we're going to the lab. Call us if you find anything!" he yelled back to Piper and Melinda as he chased after his brother.

As soon as they walked into the lab, Andy started talking a mile a minute as he always did. They'd learned early on that you don't waste time with pleasantries or you often missed all of the important information.

"The rose that was found in the victim's throat was placed there while the victim was still alive, as there was evidence of digested matter, suggesting his gag reflex was intact at the time of insertion, which was undoubtedly painful. There were no pesticides present, which isn't all that unusual nowadays, but the odd thing was there was no sign of preserving agents that most florists would use to keep the blooms fresh after they're cut. I'm not sure if that will help or not, but it seemed odd.

"The fingerprint on the card was Julianne Howard's, as you know, however the blood used to make the print was not her blood and did not match any of the other samples we have related to the case. We did a DNA test to see if that could link it back to one of the samples or point us in a different direction perhaps, but all we were able to determine is that the blood was from an unknown female. Whomever it belongs to, there were no matches in the system, but it seems unlikely that it belongs to the killer based on the amount of strength that is required to subdue and kill in this manner.

"The photographs were all printed on the same photo paper, but here's where it gets strange. The company that sold this particular paper went out of business fifteen years ago and all of these photos were printed recently.

"The photo with the woman was taken at the East Lake Forest train station. I ride by it every day on my way in to work. They recently made some renovations last year, so the photo was taken before that. I'll keep working on enhancing the image further. As far as the photos of Julianne Howard go, one was taken outside of her workplace, and the other was taken from inside of her home on the night she was murdered, it would appear, perhaps from a closet, based on the shadows in the foreground."

"Okay, take a deep breath; you're starting to turn blue," Devon stated as he shut off the voice recorder on his cell phone. He found it was the only way to get all of the details once Andy got on a roll.

"Did you check the blood from the print against Jillian Stroh?" Mason questioned.

"Not specifically no, but it would have matched up since she's already in our database. Why, do you have a theory?" Andy asked.

"No, but there has to be a connection. The victims are way too random not to mean something and apart from Jill, all of the victims were adopted."

"Are you sure Jill wasn't adopted?" Devon wondered.

"Yeah. Her dad died when she was little, but as far as I know, her mom was alive at least until she was legally an adult. For all I know of her, she could still be alive."

"Huh? So how does she fit into this puzzle?" Andy asked.

"Good question. I'm guessing the answer might be the key to his motives, though, if Jill really was his first victim," Devon answered as he looked at the papers scattered on Andy's desk.

"What if she wasn't the first victim?" Mason asked.

"We've run the MO through every database available to us. No matches before her. If he killed before, he was trying a lot harder to hide the bodies."

"Right, but play along for a minute here. Her wounds were practiced, not the kind of thing you see with a first kill. We know she was the first kill with this MO that was found, but what if he got his taste for blood by accident and then honed his craft from there?"

"Then we better hope we can figure out the when, where, why, and how of his evolution. Because otherwise, there's no telling how big his body count could be. If that's true, then he has a whole heck of a lot more than a year up on us," Devon said.

"I know. And there is no telling how many more people are on his list."

Devon and Mason were just headed out of the lab when they got a call from Melinda.

"What have you got, Mel?" Mason asked as he switched to speakerphone so they could both hear the call.

"A survivor, I think."

"Where?" Mason said as he flipped on the flashing lights while Devon pulled away from the curb.

"A couple blocks off Clark, on Belmont. Isn't that near your place?" Melinda asked.

"Is someone there now?" he asked as panic began to rise.

"Uniforms are on the way to secure the scene and Fire and Rescue has been dispatched to the location. Piper and I are about two minutes out. Evidently, the victim called 911. As I heard it, she's in bad shape but alive."

Mason could hear the blood rushing behind his ears and a cold sweat breaking out over his skin.

"Which direction? How many blocks off of Clark?" Devon shouted as he stared at his brother's sickly pallor.

Chapter 6

"East. What's your deal? About a two blocks just east of Halstead. Dr. Hovey's about forty minutes out," she said.

"Breathe man. Just breathe. It's not her, she's safe all the way down at Southport," Devon said as he squeezed Mason's shoulder.

Mason looked up as he tried to stifle his sigh of relief. It wasn't Dakota, but someone was still dying and he couldn't help the feeling of guilt over being happy that she was safe.

"You want to go check on her?" Devon asked as they pulled up to the building, right behind Piper's truck.

"No. I'm okay. Let's get this over with," Mason told him.

As they made their way into the building, Devon stopped to talk to the first officer on the scene. Mason sprinted up the stairs to see what kind of shape the victim was in and to see if he could get any kind of statement from her.

He pushed through the front door, only to find there was not one victim, but two. A male was positioned straight ahead and on the floor in front of him was a void in the shape of a small crouching person. However, drag marks indicated that the woman had pulled herself across the carpet into another part of the home where she had called 911.

Two victims at once in broad daylight and leaving a survivor weren't the only things that were different with this crime scene. The male was in a sitting position with his back against a beam, his legs secured with zip ties and a pair of scalpels embedded in his hands extended above his head; his eyelids had been taped back so aggressively that you could see the space between his eyes and the orbital bone. And his carotid and brachial arteries had both been severed. This time, no tourniquets had been applied prior to making the incisions. His mouth had also been taped shut and based on the protrusion of his throat, the calling card was undoubtedly entombed with his last dying breath. There was an additional spray pattern on the victim as well as

53

the floor surrounding him and three shallow knife wounds surrounded by substantial amounts of blood, more than he was likely to lose for wounds that shallow.

Mason went further into the home, following the trail of blood in search of the survivor, praying that she would be able to fill in the gaps before they transported her to the hospital. As he approached the kitchen, he saw one of the EMT's coming out of the room.

"How is she?" Mason asked.

The EMT just shook his head and pointed him into the kitchen. When he got there, he saw the woman lying on the floor. Her breaths were shallow and raspy as she tried and failed to pull oxygen into her lungs. There was no precision to her injuries, and she was alive, both indicating that she was either the person he blamed for whatever wrong was committed against him, or that she wasn't a part of the plan and he'd been forced to improvise when she interrupted. Her arms were covered in defensive wounds and there were four ever-expanding spirals of blood soaking her t-shirt from what appeared to be knife wounds.

As he took in her wounds, he realized the shallow wounds on the other victim were likely from the killer stabbing the woman as she leaned against the male victim. Though it would appear the wound that pierced her heart had occurred at a distance. Judging by the lack of smearing, Mason was sure that had been the final and fatal blow. It had been a miracle she'd survived as long as she had.

Mason knelt beside her and picked up her hand, "Ma'am, my name is Mason. I am with the police department. Can you tell me what happened?"

"Already here...when... I... got... here. Didn't see... but... called me 'Em...mie.' No one....calls me....that.....anymore," she said around gasps of air.

Mason looked to the EMT for explanation and he held up her ID with the name Emelie Hartrey.

"How long since you've been called 'Emmie'?"

"Fifteen...years. My dad ... called me...Emmie ...he died... fifteen years ago."

"Were you adopted after that?"

"No...my brother and....step-sister....took care of me," she answered as sobs tore from her throat, causing blood to bubble up from her lungs. Within seconds, her breathing stopped as the blood filled her airway, drowning her in her own blood, the answers they so desperately needed dying with her. Mason just sat there for a minute or two, staring at her, wondering how she fit into the puzzle and why had she been treated so differently from the other victims.

Mason stood and walked back into the living room, glancing around for more information as Devon walked into the apartment.

"How's the survivor?" he asked.

Mason shook his head before saying, "She died a few minutes ago. He went off the rails with this one. Two victims. One victim seemed to fall within his normal MO, though he bumped it up a notch, as you can see," Mason said as he pointed to the scalpels. "It looks like the second victim may have interrupted him or he'd been waiting for her to arrive, perhaps. See these shallow wounds? I think he got them as the female victim was stabbed from behind while trying to free him. Clearly, there was a significant deviation from his usual methods with the female vic. She was stabbed a number of times and was not restrained. It felt a little more...personal, like she brought out his rage. It lacked his usual precision and planning."

"Michael Hartrey, 30. The girl, I'm told, was Emelie Hartrey, 23," Devon supplied, having learned the tenant's name from the landlord and his sibling's from the responding officer a few minutes ago.

"Must be the brother then? Apparently, there is a stepsister. Emelie told me that she was raised by the two when their parents died, so she wasn't adopted and neither was Michael. Anyway, the shallow wounds have far too much blood for such superficial wounds. The spatter pattern on his body and the surrounding area suggests her fourth stab wound was the fatal blow to her heart. If it had been the first, we'd see smearing from Emelie being pushed forward while she was stabbed. We'll have to have Dr. Hovey and the lab look at each of their wounds, but I think what they'll find is three of her stab wounds will match up with her being stabbed from behind as she tried to free her brother. And we need to figure out if she was supposed to be here, or if she was lured here."

"Okay, so we'll dump their phones and check work schedules and I'll have a uniform go with CSU to Emelie's address and see if they can find anything that might indicate whether this was a social visit or something more ominous. Dr. Hovey was just pulling up when I was downstairs getting more evidence bags." Melinda said.

"Ask and you shall receive," Dr. Hovey said as she entered the room, followed by her assistant, Joe Darcy, who was pushing a gurney.

"You're going to need another one of those," Devon said, pointing to the gurney.

"I heard. What the hell happened here?" Dr. Hovey asked as she glanced around the room. "I was really hoping that perhaps the second victim would be leaving via ambulance."

Dr. Hovey's assistant quickly headed back down to the truck to get the second gurney and bag while the doc got straight down to business.

"We were, too. But the EMTs said there wasn't anything they could do."

"Well, let's take a look at her first, shall we?"

Mason led everyone into the kitchen and watched as Dr. Hovey went to work.

"How she survived long enough to call 911, let alone until you arrived is beyond me. Based on the spatter in the other room and the location of the wound, I'd say the final blow pierced her heart and probably her left lung, too. She should have bled out almost instantly. The killer was a bit hasty with her. Looks like four quick stab wounds. Let's take a look at the male victim," she said as she stood up and walked into the other room.

Mason and Devon followed.

"This was more practiced. Though the tourniquets are missing. Perhaps he had to finish him quickly if the other victim made a lot of noise? At least it appears that she was a surprise attack, so it probably wasn't the silence he's used to. These stab wounds, they look like they might line up with three of the female victims," Dr. Hovey said as she pointed to the corresponding wounds.

"Yeah. We think she was trying to free her brother when the killer stabbed her from behind, delivering the fatal blow from a distance and throwing her to the ground here," Mason said as he pointed to the void in the carpet that was surrounded by blood.

"And then he finished off the brother, Michael and got out of here," Devon finished.

"I also think that the victims knew the killer. Or at the very least, he knew them. He called the female vic 'Emmie,' a nickname that she said no one used since their parents had died," Mason added.

"Well, it looks like Michael's got your calling card. Did you find anything else yet?" she asked as she peeled the tape from his mouth, revealing the rose. His jaw was still pliant so the rose was clearly visible. Dr. Hovey carefully removed the rose in order to keep the stem intact, and passed it to Mason, who was waiting with an evidence bag.

"Not yet. We only arrived a few minutes before you did," Devon said.

"Any signs of a note?" Mason asked of the room as a whole. There were easily ten cops milling about.

"Not yet, maybe the female vic interrupted before he had the chance to leave it," Melinda said as she came into the room.

Dr. Hovey checked the area surrounding the body and Mason went into the kitchen to check around Emelie for any clues. He set the phone back in the cradle and seconds later, the phone rang.

"Hello," Mason said as he pressed the speaker. Silence filled the line as the team crowded into the entry to listen.

"Hello," he said again.

"Mason Cole, I presume," a digitally enhanced voice stated.

"This is Cole."

"It's an honor to work with you. I do hope that you are enjoying the hunt as much as I am," the voice said.

Mason looked over and saw Piper whispering on his phone, without a doubt working on tracing the call.

"I wouldn't go so far as saying an honor, no. And certainly I can think of a lot of things I'd rather be doing than hunting you."

"Perhaps. You might want to check the mail slot. You won't find the clues standing next to the girl," the voice said before the line went dead.

The team looked around, trying to figure how the killer knew they stood in the kitchen. But, there appeared to be no sightline with any of the windows.

"Have the tech unit do a search. See if he's got eyes on the place or perhaps he's listening. If he'd known she was alive, he would never have left her here." With that thought, he pushed the play button on the answering machine.

The first two messages were regarding appointments and dry cleaning. The third was Emelie.

"Hi, big brother! I'm on my way into the city. Just thought I'd give you a call and let you know I'd be there in about two hours. I can't believe you found him! Let me know if you want me to pick up some lunch on the way. Can't wait to catch up tonight! Love you."

"I guess we know why she was here," Devon thought aloud.

"I guess we do. Who do you think her brother found?" Mason added.

"I'm not sure, but I can't help wondering if maybe they went looking for something they shouldn't have. We should check the mail slot," Devon said as he and the team made their way down to the entrance. Once they popped the box open, they sifted through contents and found a mailer with nothing written on it.

Mason opened it and let the contents fall onto the counter in front of him. A second white rose with blood droplets fell free first, followed by a photograph of what appeared to be the BMW from the last photo he'd left them. This time it was totaled and smoke rose from the engine block. The male driver slumped over the wheel in a lifeless heap and a woman in the passenger seat with her hair matted to the wound against the side of her head.

"Why do you think he keeps going back to this?" Mason asked.

"I don't know, but it was important enough to show us twice," Melinda said.

The last item was a card with an inscription.

Mason read the message out loud. "Those we love don't go away; they walk beside us every day. Unseen, unheard, but always near. You left me there, so live in fear." There was a partial fingerprint in what appeared to be blood left on the upper corner of the card.

"This looks like a condolence card, written in blood. What do you think it means? And whose blood do you suppose this is?" Piper asked.

"I have no idea, but I suspect there is some significance to it." It was the only answer Mason could offer.

"Clearly, he's found his stride. Let's hope that his haste has led him to make a mistake. Otherwise, we're stuck waiting on his next move. I'm going to go monitor the CSU team and make sure the evidence gets back to the lab ASAP," Piper said as he turned to head back up to the crime scene.

"Piper, if you're going to stay here, why don't we meet up around noon. It's already almost eight, and I'm guessing it will be a few hours before you get to the lab. I'll call you if anything happens and we need you to come in sooner," Mason called after him.

"I'll stay with Piper. We'll be in touch if anything comes up tonight. Get some sleep if you can. Someone should," Melinda said before catching up to Piper.

"Mase, no offense, but you look destroyed. Want me to drop you at home?" Devon asked as they walked out to the car.

"No. I need some air. I'm just going to walk," he answered.

"Well, you know you live that way."

"Not going home. See you at 7:30? " Mason said as he headed off in the other direction.

"At the diner," Devon added, and shook his head as he got in his car and headed home for a few hours.

Kristi Loucks

Chapter 7

Mason walked into the diner and noticed it was quite busy. Judy looked up and caught his eye. "She's still at home," she said as she hurried to her next table.

As he turned back towards the street, something fluttered by into the alley beside the diner. When he got closer, he crouched down and picked up the tiny white disk. A single white rose petal sat in his hand. In his mind, he knew it was probably just an errant petal that came from a grocery store bouquet, but it didn't stop him from sprinting the remaining distance to Dakota's house.

When he arrived, he was nearly frantic and breathless. He knocked on the door twice before he heard movement and the sound of Dakota's voice as she came down the stairs. She opened the door and Mason's heart started to settle a little.

"I'm so sorry; I didn't mean to startle you. It's just been a really bad day," he said before he stepped inside and closed the door.

As he turned the lock, he felt her arms wrap around his torso. "You don't need to explain to me. I heard on the news that there was a double homicide. I figured you'd be there," she whispered.

Mason turned in her arms and pulled her against his chest as he kissed her forehead. "I need to tell you something," he said quietly.

"Why don't we sit down," she said as she led him into her living room. She picked up the phone and called Colleen to cover the prep as she sat on the couch.

He sat beside her as she turned and leaned her cheek against her hand. Mason took her free hand in his, needing the contact and fearing this conversation might be the end of whatever was brewing between them.

"Mason, I'm not going anywhere," he said as she let her other hand rest on his shoulder.

"I'm not so sure. But, I hope that's true," he said as he brushed the hair from her forehead.

"Whatever it is, you can't keep carrying it around with you."

"I told you that I had personal interest in joining the Serial Crimes Unit."

"I remember."

"About a year ago, my girlfriend, Jill, and I had moved back to the city. We wanted to be closed to Dev, so I had taken a job at the Naval Academy and she had taken a job as a social worker for special needs kids. I had been out at the Naval Academy for the day, finalizing paperwork, and was running late because of an accident at the junction. When I got home, the house was quiet. I thought maybe Jill had called Devon to go to dinner when I was late, so I made my way to the bathroom for a quick shower before I tracked them down." Mason said as he took a deep breath.

Dakota moved closer and let her hand glide up his arm until her fingers rested against his cheek. She felt a single warm tear and she knew that whatever was coming next must have been devastating to the man in front of her.

"Mason, before you say anything else, I want you to know I'm not going anywhere. Whatever you tell me, it doesn't change how I feel."

He kissed the palm of the hand that had been resting against his cheek and placed it over his heart, which was beating frantically as he took a deep breath.

"When I flipped on the light, the first thing that caught my eye was a bright red handprint against the glossy white subway tiles that covered the bathroom walls. I turned back into the hall with my heart in my throat as the bathroom light revealed several bright red boot prints heading into the bedroom, so I followed them. I pushed the door open and was immediately caught off guard by the metallic odor of fresh blood." His breath caught as the memories dragged him back to that night.

Dakota waited patiently for him to start talking again as she wiped the tears from his cheek, her heart breaking for him as she felt how much pain this still caused him.

"What I found was beyond horrific. I knew she was gone, and I'm pretty sure she died quickly, but all I could think was what if I'd gotten home on time. Could I have stopped it? Did she cry out for me to save her? I should have..." The last sentence hung between them as the emotions he'd been holding in since that night finally broke free.

Dakota moved closer and pulled Mason into her arms, rubbing a hand over his back as she whispered, "You are not to blame for this. You could never have predicted that something like that would happen. I know that I can't take away the pain, but you can't keep blaming yourself for the actions of a murderer. There is no way you could have known."

After a few minutes, Mason spoke softly. "I took the job the week after I found her. I'd been approached a month earlier when they'd spoken to Devon about it, but I declined, not wanting to immerse myself in that kind of darkness. After she died, all I had left was darkness so I took the job. Anyway, on the night that I first spoke to you in the diner, we had the first break in the case in nine months. He planted Jill's ID at the crime scene. And he's been sure to leave clues at all the subsequent crime scenes, too. Tonight, when we got the call, they told us that it was on Belmont a couple of blocks from Clark and I went into a panic. For a moment, I was frozen by this fear that he had come for you and I felt guilty when I found out it was on the East side of Clark because I was relieved and happy, knowing you were safe even though two people lost their lives tonight. What kind of person does that make me?"

"I don't think anyone would fault you for being relieved it wasn't someone you knew. I can't think of anyone who would feel any differently. That just makes you human," she said.

"I know, but then on my way here from the diner I saw something, a rose petal outside the diner and the panic set in again. That's why I was pounding on your door like a lunatic. I was so afraid of losing you and all I could think was that I haven't even kissed you properly," he whispered as his hands brushed against the sides of her neck.

"Mason, you can kiss me anytime that you want. I have no plans to resist you, in fact..."

Before she could finish her thought, she felt his thumb brush her lower lip as he moved closer. His left hand swept up into her hair just as his lips pressed softly against hers. At first, the kiss was an unhurried exploration, but then Dakota's fingernails brushed softly against Mason's scalp and the air started to crackle around them.

Mason carefully lifted Dakota into his lap and let his hands travel, allowing his left hand to find its way up to cradle her head and his right to the small of her back to leverage her tiny frame flush against his body without a centimeter of space between them.

For Mason, the kiss was like nothing he'd ever felt before. His heart was fluttering in his chest like a caged hummingbird as he felt her open to him. She tasted of peppermint and her skin smelled of peaches as it warmed under his touch. His lungs burned as they begged for air until he finally gave in, following the scent of her skin as he kissed the smooth column of her neck, allowing his teeth to graze her ever so gently. He laughed as she sighed, making a sound like a content little kitten.

"God, that wasn't at all what I expected for a first kiss," he whispered as he smiled against the hollow of her throat.

"Mmm, I knew you would be a good kisser. You are far too attentive not to be," she whispered.

"How do you figure?" he asked as he kissed her neck once more.

"I haven't been with enough men to make a fair comparison, but most just simply don't know how to be with a blind woman. You're different, though. You seem to understand my world intuitively. You walk me home, but you don't lead me home. You talk to me when you approach so that I can gauge where you are. These are things that even people who have spent their whole lives around me sometimes neglect to do. You don't treat me like there is a disadvantage; you just level the playing field so you can treat me like anyone else," she said.

"I don't want to treat you like anyone else. I want you to know you're important to me," he said, taken aback by her last statement.

"Mason, don't you see? Most people have to learn that I can do things for myself. You've never treated me like a helpless blind woman. And that means more than any grand gesture ever could. You see me as capable. Hell, most people, when they introduce me, say things like, 'This is Dakota. She's blind.' When I met your brother, you never even mentioned it."

"You are so much more than a blind woman. Anyone who can't see that you are beautiful, kind, smart, and driven would have to be far more impaired than you are blind. I know women who have perfect vision that can't see the world the way that you do. So, no, when I look at you, I don't see 'blind.' I see a woman who appreciates the world in different ways. In ways that I would like to see the world and most of all, I see a lightness in the world around me that hasn't been there in a long time, and I can't help but think that you might be responsible for that. For that matter, Devon is sure that you're responsible," Mason said as he smiled against her cheek.

"Well, I'm glad that I won't have to win him over then. Because I want to be a part of your life, if you'll let me," she whispered.

"You had Devon with a blueberry muffin." Mason laughed. "But, you had me at 'hello.' And that kiss didn't hurt either. I want to be a part of your life, too."

"You could stay here tonight, if you want."

"Dakota, I don't want to rush you into this. I don't want to mess up whatever we have going here," he said.

"I know. And I don't want that either, but I don't want you to go home alone."

"So what do you propose?" he asked her.

"I have a king-sized bed and I trust you not to do anything that would make it uncomfortable. Stay with me," she said as she stood up and held out her hand.

Mason took her hand and allowed her to lead him upstairs to her bedroom. He looked around when he entered the room, noticing the stained glass moon casting a golden glow surrounded by blues and greens in her window. He traced its edge with one finger, wondering how she would look as the glass cast colored shadows against her skin.

"My mother made that for me when I was little; I liked all of the colors. It's one of my last visual memories," Dakota said as her hands gripped the hem of his sweatshirt, helping him ease it over his head.

When her hands came to his vest and holster, she hesitated, so he pulled the Velcro straps and set the vest on the dresser along with his gun and badge.

"They're just precautions. It's not like we get shot at every day. I was in such a hurry to get to you that I for—"

"I'm glad. I want you to be safe," she interrupted before pulling his t-shirt from the waist of his jeans. "I might have an old pair of my dad's sweatpants if you want."

"I can sleep in my boxers and t-shirt if you're okay with that."

"Whatever's comfortable is fine with me," she said as she walked towards the closet. "There should be an extra toothbrush in the cabinet beside the sink."

Mason flipped on a light in the bathroom and noticed that everything was neatly arranged. He opened the cabinet and found a brand new toothbrush. He quickly washed up and brushed his teeth before heading back into the bedroom.

A moment later, Dakota came out of the closet with clothes in her hand, heading into the bathroom as she said, "I'll be done in a minute."

Mason smiled as he looked at the stained glass, thinking about Dakota as a little girl. When he heard the bathroom door open, his heart began to trip even before he turned around.

"Over here," he whispered as she moved towards the sound of his voice.

When she stood in front of him, he couldn't help but lay his hands on the exposed skin between her shoulder blades while he pressed his lips against hers. When he felt her hands skim across his stomach beneath the hem of his shirt, his heart felt like it was about to burst from his chest.

"I think maybe we should slow this down a little," he whispered despite every nerve ending he had protesting vehemently to this plan.

She smiled and nodded as she led him to the bed, turning the covers down as she climbed in before holding them up for him to join her. She turned to her side so that they faced each other and said, "I'm sorry for all that you've lost. I can't even imagine how that felt. But, I'm really glad that you found comfort in my little diner."

"Me, too," he whispered.

She turned to her other side and he closed his eyes, but before sleep had a chance to claim him, he felt her hand reach back for his as she motioned for him to close the distance between them. He breathed her in as he wrapped his arms around her and pulled her back against his chest before sleep finally swept over them.

He vaguely recalled the alarm clock going off around four and Dakota speaking softly into the phone, but it wasn't until the light warmed his back that he realized he was still wrapped around a very warm and very beautiful woman.

"Mmmm. Good morning," he whispered as he stretched.

"Yes, it is." She smiled. "I haven't played hooky from work in five years. It felt really good to sleep in."

He glanced at the clock and noticed that it was still only six fifteen in the morning. "To most people, six fifteen in the morning wouldn't be considered sleeping in." He laughed.

"It is for me. And it didn't suck to wake up in your arms either," she whispered as her hand glanced over his stomach where his shirt had ridden up.

Without thought, she let her fingers coast over the ridges of his abs until she felt a thin line of soft hair that stopped a few inches above the waist of his boxers. When that realization hit, her hand stilled as her cheeks flushed with embarrassment. Before she could pull away, Mason put her hand over his thundering heart and pulled her down for a kiss.

When they were good and breathless, Mason pulled back and said, "Dakota, whatever you think you did wrong, stop. I don't want you to put your guard up because you think I'll get freaked out. I'm not going to do that. Even though your hands on me just now were the best kind of torture, I'm not going to read anything into it. No expectations. I would love to know what you're thinking inside that pretty little head, though."

She smiled. "That's the problem. I wasn't thinking about anything, I was just appreciating your freakishly toned abs when all of a sudden I realized what you must have been thinking."

"I was thinking, 'holy crap her hands feel amazing on my skin,' for the record. Admittedly, parts of my body may have been thinking something else, but my mother taught me to always use the brain that's between my ears." He laughed.

Dakota laughed out loud and Mason couldn't help but notice how nice it felt to talk to her about his mom. He hadn't shared his memories of her with many people, but he couldn't help but think how much his mom would have liked Dakota.

"I wish I could have met your mom. Judging by her sons, I think I would have liked her an awful lot."

"I know she would have liked you too," Mason told her as he leaned in and kissed her softly before climbing out of the bed. "Can I cook you breakfast for once? I make a mean omelet."

"That sounds amazing."

"I'll find my way around the kitchen. Why don't you take a shower and I'll walk you to the diner after breakfast," he said as he pulled his jeans on and carried the rest of his things downstairs.

As he was getting the pan warmed up, he heard the shower turn on and Nina Simone's sultry voice on the stereo. He smiled as he remembered his mom playing this album to death when he was little. In that moment, he hummed along as he realized he was feeling pretty good, too.

By seven, Mason and Dakota were walking down Belmont on their way to the diner when his phone chirped.

Don't think I wouldn't know that you didn't come home last night...

Mason laughed as he said, "Evidently, my brother decided I shouldn't be alone last night either. Looks like we're busted."

"Tell him that I'm better company."

"I think I will."

Mason dialed his brother, "Dakota told me to tell you that she's better company."

"She did? Well, I take it that means you got to kiss the girl finally? Anything else I should know about?" Devon joked.

"Yes. Yes and nothing that I plan to tell you, big brother."

Dakota laughed at their easy banter just as Devon opened the door to the diner for the pair. "You, my friend, need to shower and change lest you want to invite the inquisition. Don't worry; I'll keep Dakota busy while you're away."

Mason looked at his brother like he'd sprouted another head while Dakota simply laughed and said, "I'll be fine. I'm sure Devon could use some coffee and a cinnamon roll."

"I was just thinking the same thing. Then you can tell me what's going on with the two of you because he won't tell me anything!" Devon said as he put his arm around her shoulder and winked at Mason.

Mason ran home, showered, and changed in record time, but it didn't stop Devon from chatting with Dakota in the meantime.

"I'm only kidding, you know," Devon said.

"About?" she asked.

"You don't have to tell me anything. I can see everything that I need to know on your faces," he answered as Molly dropped off two cups of coffee and a warm cinnamon roll for the two to share. They thanked her and she went to the next table.

Dakota asked, "What do you see?"

"Smiles. It's been a long time since I've seen him smile at all. He looks happy when you're around. Heck, for the first time in almost a year, he looks happy when you're not around, too. I think you're to blame for that as well. And I can't help but notice that you look happy, too."

"I am. He's a really good guy and he makes me feel accepted and whole, I guess. He doesn't see a blind girl. He sees Dakota." She smiled brightly as she talked about him.

"Sweetheart, anyone who doesn't see Dakota is afflicted with something that is far more debilitating than blindness. It's called 'ignorance.'"

Dakota put her hand out and Devon covered it with his as he watched her rub a lone tear onto her sleeve. "Mason said something quite similar," she whispered.

"Great minds." He laughed. "Listen, I don't know how much he's shared with you, but…"

"He told me about Jill. How he found her and why he took the job," Dakota interrupted.

"Good. That's really good. He was worried about how you would take it."

"I knew there was something haunting him. I could feel it. When he came to see me last night, I could tell that his thoughts were burning a hole in his chest. So I did the only thing I could. I listened. And do you know what I learned?"

"What's that?"

"Your brother is incredibly strong to have survived what he did, but beyond that, not many men would be able to pick up the pieces and go to the gates of hell looking for the devil that broke him."

Devon smiled. "I never really thought about it like that, but you're right. I've spent so much time worrying about the possibility of a fall out, that I thought it was about revenge. And I'm sure to some extent it is for all of us really, but at the same time he's been putting his life back together and I've been too caught up in the worst case scenarios to see it."

"No, you've just been worried about your little brother," she whispered.

Devon smiled as he glanced out the window and saw Mason whistling to himself as he crossed the street and reached for the front door.

"Better?" Mason said as he sat down and pulled Dakota in closer to his side before he kissed her cheek.

Molly came over, set a cup of coffee down in front of him, and topped off the other two cups.

"Yes, but if you keep on whistling a happy tune it was probably a waste of time because Piper and Melinda will know something's up anyway."

Mason laughed out loud. "Yeah, about that. I was thinking maybe we could have them meet us here for lunch. They aren't due in until later so we can head out and get updates from the lab and come back. Then I can introduce them to Dakota. We've got to eat lunch anyway. Dakota, is that okay with you?"

"Of course."

"Wow. Whatever you did to him last night, keep doing it," Devon said.

Mason was about to protest when he heard Devon yelp and caught the little smirk on Dakota's lips.

"You sure you can't see because your aim is like a freaking sniper," he said as he rubbed his shin.

"You make it too easy when you sit over there laughing at your own jokes," she said with a sweet little smile.

"She's got a point," Mason said as he gave in to the temptation and kissed her right there in the middle of the diner.

"We should get going, but I'll see you in a few hours if you're really okay with meeting Melinda and Piper."

"I'm looking forward to it," she said as he kissed her cheek and walked their dishes to the counter. She also heard Molly protest as he'd obviously slipped a ten between the plates again, knowing Dakota had instructed her not to take his money from him the other day.

Devon put a hand on her shoulder as he leaned down and whispered, "Thanks for being there for him last night. You have no idea how thankful I am that he ended up in your diner all those months ago." Then he surprised her by kissing her cheek before Mason returned and did the same.

"See you in a little while."

"I'll hold our table," she said as he walked out the front door.

"Dakota, he is hotter than hell and he looks at you like he wants to lick the frosting off the cupcake." Molly all but squealed happily.

"Oh, Molly! I think you should hang out with Devon a little more. I might have expected that from him. That was just wrong!" Dakota scolded.

As she turned to walk away, Molly heard her snicker as she shot back, "I'd like to do more than lick the frosting off."

Both of them laughed as they went about preparing for the upcoming lunch rush.

Chapter 8

Devon waited until Mason had closed his door and stepped on the gas before he started talking.

"So, I take it last night went…well?"

"It did."

"And you told her about Jill?"

"Clearly you already know that I did, and it went much better than I could have hoped."

"Dakota may have mentioned it. For the record, she's pretty amazing, in case you hadn't already made that discovery."

"Oh, I did. I was so afraid to tell her, but she never even flinched. I didn't tell her the gory details, but even the Cliff Notes are pretty bad."

"Agreed. So. You stayed at her place. Get any sleep?"

"I did. So did she, by the way, since I know that's going to be your next question."

"Interesting. So, you slept in Dakota's bed with her and nothing happened?"

"Yep. Nothing happened. Now, drop it."

Devon watched his brother out of the corner of his eye for a moment before he let the conversation drop, for the time being. He would simply have to enlist reinforcements once the rest of the team met Dakota.

"You should text Melinda and Piper about lunch before we head in."

Mason nodded and quickly fired off a text to each of them.

They pulled into the parking lot of the forensic lab a few minutes later and headed up to see what they had been able to uncover.

Robin was working today, which was notably better than dealing with Andy first thing in the morning.

"Good morning," Robin said as they entered the lab.

"Good morning," they returned.

"First of all, I understand you've been holding out on me. Melinda was telling us that you have the hook up for some outstanding cinnamon rolls. Just keep in mind that the lab is fueled on sugar and caffeine the next time you drop in."

"Noted," Mason said with a smile. "What have you got for us?"

"Well, the trace got us a big fat load of nothing. It was a burn phone. And there was no evidence of surveillance equipment in the apartment, so it was likely an educated guess since it was the only landline in the house and he probably has access to a police scanner, which would have told him that the woman survived."

"Okay. That makes sense," Devon thought aloud.

"Dr. Hovey sent the autopsy results and evidence about an hour ago. Apparently, this knife tip got lodged in her third rib and broke off. Hovey thinks that it may have temporarily slowed the blood flow, allowing her to survive long enough to make the 911 call. However, as soon as it dislodged, the wound to both her heart and lung were no longer blocked by the blade. It appears that she bled out rapidly once that occurred. Dr. Hovey was certain that the female victim would never have made it to the ER," she said as she handed Mason a jar with the evidence inside.

"Do you know anything about the knife itself?"

"Yes. It was the type of utility knife used by someone who does a lot of gardening. It is heavy duty and has a serrated blade on one side with numbers to mark soil depth running down the center of the blade. I can't give you an exact brand, but it appears to have been something the killer brought with him, since we found no gardening tools of any kind in the apartment or the outlying buildings."

Robin slid her chair over to one of the machines, pulling up another set of results.
"Piper told me your guy has a thing for roses, so I checked over the clothing, looking for any particulates that might have been transferred from the knife and found a sandy residue where the hilt of the blade touched her. The sand and mineral content is consistent with Racine County in South Eastern Wisconsin."

"Well, at least that means we're not on a nationwide manhunt, but that still leaves a lot of rocks to turn over," Devon said.

"I'm sorry. I wish I could give you more on that front. I do have some good news, though."

"What's that?"

"The mystery of the BMW is solved. As you know, the driver was Walter Hartrey and his wife Amber was the passenger killed in the accident. They were the parents of your victims, Emelie and Michael. Amber also had a daughter from a previous relationship named Alyssa Marchand, but we have not been able to locate her as next of kin."

"Keep looking, for all we know, she could be in danger as well," Mason said.

"We have our best people digging into it. There was one last thing; the rose that was found in the mailer and the rose found in the victim's throat appear to be the same type of roses found with the previous victims. And once again, there was not a preserving agent present or any sign of pesticides. I'm not sure how that helps just yet, but it's worth mentioning. That's about everything, I think," Robin said as she looked to Mason and Devon for questions.

"Based on the photo of the accident, it looks like there was another car. Any info on the driver? Survivors?"

"Oh, Yes. Her name is Angela Forrester, or it was at the time. I've been unable to locate her thus far, but by all accounts, she walked away from the accident relatively unharmed. Evidently, she was on her way to pick up her ten-year-old daughter and decided to make a stop off at the friendly neighborhood tavern."

"DUI?"

"Probably, but nothing ever came of it because there was a malfunction with the traffic light."

"Well, let us know if anything else comes up. We'll go over it with Kade and Torello and see if anything stands out. Maybe Melinda can work her voodoo on the computer and find Angela Forrester and Alyssa Marchand, too," Devon offered.

"Thanks for your help," Mason said as they made their way back to the car.

"Any word from Piper or Melinda? Are we headed to the diner or the office?"

Mason checked his cell phone and saw three missed text messages. Two from Piper, and a third from Melinda.

Y in god's name RU texting me @O dark thirty in the am when we're not on til 12?

Wait, THE diner? I'M IN.

If I can meet the mystery woman, I will forgive you for waking me up…see you at lunch.

"Looks like the diner," Mason said with a smile.

"You're kidding; no snide remarks from Piper?"

"Other than wondering why he got a text at O dark thirty, nope."

"Huh. It was like nearly eight when you texted him, wasn't it?"

"Have you ever been in his house? He lives like a vampire with his blackout shades and dark walls," Mason shared.

"Yeah, I suppose he does live like a bit of a diva."

A few minutes later, Devon parked down the street from the diner. Mason smiled when he walked in and saw two tables pushed together with a handwritten RESERVED sign.

Devon went ahead and sat down while Mason went in search of Dakota. He found her in the kitchen with the music playing softly in the background while she portioned ingredients for her prep.

"Have I been gone long enough for you to miss me?" he asked as he moved towards her.

"I think you have," she said as she held her arms out in the direction of his voice.

As soon as his arms surrounded her, he met her with a kiss that made her forget all about his absence or the chaos of the diner at noon on a Thursday. A time that she regularly avoided, since crowds made it harder to navigate the diner unassisted, but today she'd made an exception.

"Is everyone out there?" she asked.

"Probably, but I'm not ready to share you yet," he said as he held onto her.

"Okay, so long as you're prepared for the inquisition," she said with a smile.

"It's coming no matter what time we show up out there. I figured I might as well enjoy some time with you," he said as he gave her one last kiss. "I suppose we should get out there."

Mason wrapped his arm around her when she stiffened at the sound of the crowd and led her to the table, allowing her to slide into the booth before he slid in beside her. Before he turned to his friends he whispered, "I'll always look out for you in a crowd."

"Guys, this is Dakota Shelton. She's responsible for the extra ten pounds you'll be bitching about next month."

"So you're the reason I'll be going to the gym twice a day. It's a pleasure to finally meet you," Melinda said.

"Mase, I can see why you've been hiding her," Piper said.

"It's nice to meet you both," she said.

They all chatted for a moment until Molly came over with menus and a basket of bread. She set down five glasses of water and four menus.

"I guess you wouldn't need a menu, since you probably know it backwards and forward. What's your favorite thing?" Piper asked.

Mason smiled.

"I've actually never seen our menu, but the best things by far, at least in my opinion, are the chicken and wild rice soup and the southwest chicken salad with the house made chili lime dressing," she answered.

The first part of her comment didn't click until Melinda noticed Mason pushing her water glass until it rested against her hand. Dakota smiled and said, "Thanks."

Piper looked on, confused, as Mason and Devon had a laugh until Dakota decided to let him in on the secret, "I let Judy handle the graphic design. I can bake like nobody's business, but a blind girl and graphic design just don't go together."

"Ah. Makes sense then why you'd pick this one over a guy like me then," Piper said.

"Oh, you know it would never work between us. I just don't think there's enough room for you, me, and that enormous ego," Dakota said with a fake frown.

"Oh boy. She's going to fit right in!" Melinda said as the entire group busted out laughing.

They talked and joked throughout lunch, enjoying the same easy banter that she'd come to expect from Mason and his brother. By the time they'd finished, the lunch rush had died down to a steady trickle.

"Well, I think we should head back into the office," Devon said as he stood up.

Everyone stood and started gathering their coats as Dakota began to clear the table until she felt Mason's hand on hers. He set the dishes in the bus tub near the kitchen and rejoined the group.

"I'll see you back there in a bit. Call me if anything comes up," Mason told his brother.

Devon nodded and followed Melinda and Piper out.

"You're not going with them?"

"No. They can manage without me for an afternoon, and they'll call if they need to. I wanted to make sure that you got home okay."

"Mase, you don't have to do that."

"No, but I want to."

With that cleared up, Mason and Dakota helped Molly clean up before he helped Dakota get her coat on and took her hand, leading her out to the street.

"I guess both of us are playing hooky for a little while today," Mason said as he wrapped his arm around her shoulder.

"It's not quite the same. Though you won't hear me complain," she told him.

"No. I guess it's not, but we've taken the evidence as far as it can take us for the moment. Besides, there are dozens of people working this case now, so it's not exactly being neglected. If there is one thing that I've learned in the last year, it's that you never know what tomorrow is going to bring. I don't want my job to be the only thing I have at the end of the day. And since I'm being honest, I'd really like to spend some more time with you."

She nodded as she leaned into his side and they walked the rest of the way to her place in silence.

When they stepped inside, Mason felt Dakota shiver in his arms.

"Are you cold?" he asked.

"Freezing."

"Come here," he said as he took her hand and led her into the living room. He stretched out against the back of the couch as he made room for her to curl up against his chest, pulling the blanket down around them.

"Better?" he whispered against her ear.

She nodded and said, "You're like my own personal space heater."

He laughed as her fingers wound into his hair. "Can I still kiss you anytime that I want?"

"Mmmm. Please," she hummed as his lips touched the hollow of her neck.

"One of these days you might regret saying that." He laughed.

"Unlikely," she whispered.

Mason pulled her back against his chest and the pair slept peacefully for the next hour. As with most good things in Mason's world, however, their peace was interrupted.

Mason cleared his throat as he picked up the call that had been bleating in his ear, "Mason here."

"Are the pieces starting to fall into place yet?" said the distorted voice on the other end.

"Should they be?" Mason asked as he started the voice recorder. Mason muted the call and asked for Dakota's phone to text Devon as he listened.

"Well, it really depends on who is looking at the clues. I'm willing to give you a free tip because I am feeling generous."

"What's that?" Mason asked.

"My next victim is part of the family."

"Yours or mine?"

"She might have been yours, but fate was unkind to you, wasn't she? It's not the blood ties that bind, but rather the blood ties that unravel."

"Why so cryptic?"

"If I was ready for this to end, I would send you an invitation to my grand finale, but I'm just getting started," the voice said as the caller disconnected.

By the time Mason had ended the call, Devon was pounding on the door.

"Take it easy, man. I said he called; not that he came over for cocktails."

"Mase. Stop joking around! We traced the call. It came from a call box around the corner."

Chapter 9

Mason immediately put his arm around Dakota, who looked visibly shaken by that statement.

"Did you tape the call?" Devon asked as Piper and Melinda came in with two of the cops who had been watching the house.

"Yes. He spoke in riddles. The next victim is family that might have been mine, whatever that means. It was past tense so I don't think he means anyone that's currently in my life."

Mason decided it would just be easier to play the recording for them.

"I know this isn't my place, but is he talking about Jill's family? I mean, you cared for her, so it stands to reason he might believe you would make her a part of your family one day. So could it be her family?" Dakota asked.

Piper and Melinda looked at Mason in shock as he'd barely shared the circumstances of Jill's death with them and they had been working the case.

"Mase, do you know any of her family?" Devon asked.

"No. Jill didn't talk about them much. I know her dad died when she was little and she'd lost touch with her mom, but I don't remember her saying she was dead. I tried to locate her when Jill died, but I didn't have enough information to go on. She didn't even attend the funeral," he said as he kissed Dakota on the cheek.

"Melinda, Piper, see what you can dig up on Jill's parents. I think her mom's name was Anna, but I'm not sure. Dev and I will take Dakota to the diner and put together a transcript of the call. Maybe something else will stand out. I want two units outside of Dakota's house and the diner at all times."

"Mase, even if you aren't going to stay there, we should put units on your place. This guy has got a major jones for you for some reason and I think it would be a good idea to keep an eye on things."

"Okay, but I don't think he's coming after me just yet. He's not finished, and in spite of his obvious instability, I think he understands if he comes after me now, he's going to be at his end game. There's no way he intends to walk away from that confrontation."

"Agreed, but we should still do what we can to keep him out of our personal space, yours especially."

Everyone made their way to their respective destinations without incident.

They'd spent the week picking apart the phone call and the life of Jillian Stroh, but so far, they had made no progress in locating Jill's mother, if she was even still alive.

The Reaper had remained quiet, but unfortunately, the media had finally caught wind of the moniker that he'd assigned to himself. Reporters, hungry for a sound bite, now surrounded the station and Mason was the one they were after.

Devon and Mason were walking to the car as torrents of questions were fired in their direction.

"Lt. Commander Cole, is there any truth to the rumor that the Rose Red Reaper has been in contact with you?"

"Do you feel that your life is in danger?"

"Has he been linked to the murder of Jillian Stroh? Is it true that she was the first victim?"

"Why haven't you issued an alert? Don't you think that the people of this city deserve to know if they are in danger?"

"With all due respect, ma'am, the last time I checked, it was my job to make sure the people of this city remained safe. This 'Reaper' is not after the city at large; he seems to have a very specific agenda and yes, I seem to be a part of that agenda. As far as a warning to the people of this city, I can tell you what is generally always true; stay in groups. Don't go out alone at night and be mindful of who you invite into your home. We have tripled our patrols and we are doing the best that we can to stay ahead of this and put a stop to the person responsible," Mason said.

"Are you concerned for your girlfriend?" one of the younger reporters asked.

Devon could see Mason was near the point of implosion for the young reporter's invasion into his private life, and the fear that any mention of Dakota could put a spotlight on her that would prove too tempting for the Reaper.

"You know what? No more questions!" Devon yelled as he dragged his brother back to the car.

As the doors slammed, Mason started to lose it. "I can't let him get anywhere near her. I wish I could send her far away from here and keep her safe, but the truth is I can't let her go. Even though I know she's safer as far from me as she can get."

"Mase, that's just not true. We have people on her around the clock and she's barely out of your sight when you're not working."

"I know. And I know she would have a fit if I tried to send her away. I think she's more worried about me than I am about her," Mason confided to his brother.

"Quite honestly, I am too. You need to take a step back. This can't be all on you, all the time. Maybe you should get out and do something. Hell, I'll tail you if it'll make you feel better. You said it yourself, though. He isn't going to come for you until he's ready to end it."

Mason nodded.

"You can go ahead and say it. 'You're right, Dev. Dakota deserves a night with Mason and not Lt. Commander Cole. Thank you for always having my back,'" Devon said as he poked his brother in the ribs.

"Would you just settle for, 'you're right, Dev'?"

"I guess. But only because Dakota deserves to see the guy that would walk her to and from work like a kid with a crush for a night."

"Hey, I still walk her to and from work."

"Yeah, with one hand on the trigger and laser eyes."

"Fine. But, I want you and Piper on our detail then. I'm serious."

"Anything for Dakota," Devon added just to rile his brother.

"Ha ha, Dev. Take me to my place so that I can get everything set up. You and Piper can wait for me at the diner around six."

"No offense, little brother, but we'll wait for you outside your place around five."

"Fine."

Mason called Dakota as soon as he walked through his door, then proceeded to run around his place, picking up anything that wasn't supposed to be on the floor and trying to make sure obstacles were at a minimum. He was nervous about having Dakota at his place, but he had specific plans in mind and it wouldn't work anyplace else.

Once he had everything ready in the kitchen, he ran upstairs to take a fast shower and put clean sheets on his bed. He thought they'd probably go back to Dakota's since she was more comfortable there, but just in case.

As he put the last pillow on the bed, he smiled as he thought of how much he looked forward to just sleeping beside her. He'd never really thought much about it, but with her, everything felt different. There was a comfort between them, but there was always an underlying current of electricity that was just waiting for one of them or both of them to green light it. So far, they were both being pretty cautious, but Mason knew that the cord was going to snap at some point.

With that thought sitting prominently in his subconscious, Mason quickly adjusted the temperature on his shower to a colder setting. His nerves were starting to jump as he worried that maybe she wouldn't like what he'd been planning ever since he'd asked her on a date several weeks earlier. While they'd spent every night together since he'd shared Jill's story, they hadn't had the chance to actually have their date.

He knew the second he stepped outside of his house, he would catch shit from his brother, but he'd gone ahead and shaved before he got dressed in a pair of khakis and a button down underneath his favorite sweater for the evening. It was something that he never did, but Dev and Piper used to refer to it as an illegal maneuver because the dimples were out in full force and it pretty much meant all the women in the bar would fall into his near gravitational pull when they were younger. If he'd had the least bit of interest, it would still work now, but there wasn't a woman in the city he cared to impress other than Dakota Shelton.

These days, she was the only one he noticed and while she appreciated his dimples, he'd never really needed them to pull her in. Mason headed back downstairs to the kitchen to make sure that he'd remembered everything for the dinner he'd planned. He'd managed to get everything started earlier so that all he had left to do was warm everything up and serve it. He knocked on Dev's window and Piper rolled it down just as he tossed his cell phone in the car.

"You get to babysit the phone tonight. If anything major happens, call the house phone. Otherwise, you can assume we'll call you if we need anything," he said with a wink as he walked to the diner.

A unit tailed him all the way there and waited out front. Melinda had stuck with Dakota all afternoon, making sure she got to the diner to meet Mason since he had other arrangements to make.

"Hello, beautiful," Mason said as he walked up to the counter where Melinda, Judy, and Molly were chatting with Dakota. She was dressed in black skinny jeans and boots with a sweater, comfortable and warm just as he'd suggested.

"Hey, cupcake!" Melinda said as they all started laughing, all except for Dakota, whose cheeks flamed.

Molly had just let the cat out of the bag regarding Mason looking at Dakota like he wanted to lick the frosting off the cupcake and of course she had to share Dakota's response.

"Cupcake? Really, Mel."

"Just trying it out. But, you do clean up really nicely," she said.

"Thank you. I had to try and look like I belong in Dakota's league," he said as he kissed her cheek.

A chorus of "aws" sounded as Mason went to grab Dakota's coat. He noticed she had a small overnight bag as well, and he couldn't help smiling at the thought of her in his home.

He returned and slipped her coat over her shoulders, pulling it closed to keep her warm on their walk.

"Did you get my bag?" she asked.

"I've got it right here. Anything else?" he asked her.

"No. I think that's all," she said as he slipped his arm around her shoulder and kissed her before they headed to his place.

Once again, the patrol car followed until they arrived at his place, where Devon and Piper said a quick "hello" before Mason escorted Dakota inside.

"Want a quick tour? Not that I plan on straying too far away," he asked.

"Sure," she said. Learning a new environment was always an adventure, but she trusted Mason to help her with the surroundings.

"Okay, you're in my entry right now. How about I show you around this floor since I need to do some stuff in the kitchen? I'll show you the rest later."

He showed her where everything was and told her how many steps there were between various obstacles. She'd known he was different the first time he'd walked her home from the diner, but so far, he'd continuously made it harder for her to envision her life without him in it. Apart from feeling safe when he was around, she also found that he was the kindest and most considerate man she'd met in a long time.

He handed her a beer and got her situated across from him on a bar stool while he started to work on their dinner. She could smell fragrant limes and curry when she came in so she knew he'd gone with Thai, which was one of her favorites. What she hadn't expected was that he'd be cooking.

"I didn't know you were going to cook," she said.

"Originally, I was going to take you out. But I figured if we had to wait for things to calm down with the media, we'd never go on the date I'd been promising. And I'll admit, I was always planning on finishing the night here anyway. A surprise for later," he whispered.

"No hints?"

"Afraid not, but I have something for you. Hold on, I'll be right back," he said.

She heard him unwrapping something in what she remembered was the dining room off the kitchen for a moment and when he returned he was followed by the sweet scent of jasmine.

"These are for you. I have a vase, too. I was going to put them in your bedroom, or mine if you want to stay here," he said as he handed her the bouquet.

He watched as she closed her eyes and inhaled the perfume of the flowers in her hands, a wide smile of appreciation on her face. "They're lovely. Thank you."

"You're lovely," he said, kissing her softly before returning to the stove.

"Where did you learn to cook Thai?" she asked.

"Before I joined the SEALS, I was stationed near Thailand for sixteen months. We spent a fair amount of time at port and enjoyed a lot of the culture. I spent a lot of time visiting the markets and eventually found someone who taught me a little bit about curry and Thai noodles. My repertoire is limited, but what I know is good enough that I had to promise leftovers to Dev and Piper in order to keep them away."

Dakota laughed. "No wonder they were on such good behavior. Do they have to sit in the car for the entire shift?"

"No. I'll let them in later. They can stay in the basement guest room. I think two floors away should be adequate." He laughed.

A few minutes later, Mason filled up two bowls for Dev and Piper and called them in. Dakota laughed when he portioned two more bowls and told them to stay out of their space or he'd lock them out for the rest of the night. Then, he helped Dakota up two and a half flights of stairs, promising to show her around after dinner. She felt the cold air for a moment as he opened the door and realized he'd brought her up to a private rooftop and then she felt heated air cascade around them.

"Not to worry, I just cranked the heaters and we've got blankets, too," he said as he led her over to a giant overstuffed lounger.

Once she was comfortable, he handed her a bowl. He loved to watch her as she enjoyed every aspect of the dish. The spice of the curry and the fragrant lime, they were things that he found he'd appreciated more since he'd met her.

"Mmmm. This is delicious. If you ever decide to quit your day job, I know a diner that would love to have you." She smiled.

"I might not quit my day job, but I wouldn't mind spending time in the kitchen with you," he said as he swiped a bit of curry from her lip with his thumb.

"It's amazing, but probably not the sexiest food to eat, huh?" She laughed as she self-consciously rubbed her lip too.

Mason set their bowls down and leaned forward so that they were practically sharing the same breath of air. When she felt his lips on hers, all of her self-conscious thoughts evaporated.

"There is not a single thing about you that isn't sexy, just so we're clear," he said as his lips ghosted over her earlobe.

She practically purred as his words vibrated over her skin. "God, you have no idea just how incredible you make me feel," she whispered.

"Oh, I think I can relate. My heart hasn't stopped pounding since I left you this morning," he said, pressing her hand to his chest. "Ready for your surprise?"

"I hope so." She laughed.

She felt him reach into his pocket and realized it was a remote as Adele's "One and Only" filled the space around them.

"You said you loved to dance as long as there wasn't a crowd. I hope that this will suffice," he whispered as he pulled her close before stealing a kiss while they moved to the music. The kiss was thorough and languid while he enjoyed the way she fit into the shelter of his arms.

When the next song came on, Dakota felt warm all over hearing Adele's version of Bob Dylan's "To Make You Feel My Love." She knew that her heart was lost to this man and there was no way she would ever be the same without him.

A tear slipped down her cheek as the thought settled in around her until she felt his hand under her chin. "I think I fell for you the first time we spoke and I've fallen a little harder with each breath. You somehow managed to un-break my shattered heart and it's all yours now. I love you Dakota," he said as he kissed the tears from her cheek.

"Well, thank God we're in agreement. Because it's not going to be possible to un-love you, Mason Cole." She laughed as Mason took her hand and led her back to the lounger. He spread a blanket out beneath the heaters before they lay back with her head pressed against his heart.

"Are you warm enough?" he asked softly.

"Mmm-hmm. Perfect," she whispered as she kissed his jaw, letting her fingers appreciate his unusually smooth skin. "Don't take this the wrong way, but I kind of like it when you don't shave."

"It doesn't scratch you too much?" he asked.

"A little, but it just fits you. I like the roughness against my skin," she said on a sigh as she felt his teeth graze the skin below her earlobe.

"Can we take this inside?" he whispered.

"Yes, please."

Mason stood and lifted her from the lounger as he switched off the heaters and lights on his way to the door and grabbed their bowls. He helped her down the stairs to his bedroom and set her on the edge of the bed. "Wait right there," he said as he took the dishes and left the room.

He took the steps two at a time to the main floor to put the dishes away and grab her overnight bag. What he didn't expect was to find Piper and Dev camped out on the couch, watching a movie.

"Wasn't expecting to see you for a few more hours," Dev said.

"You two can stay, as long as you stay down here or in the guest suite in the basement. I'm not kidding. I don't even want to know you're here," he told them with a smile.

"Oh, relax. We'll behave. Anything not to sit in the car all night," Piper said as he watched Mason pick up the bag and her flowers and head back up the stairs.

"I can smell the jasmine from here."

"Let me show you around in case you need to get up in the middle of the night," he said taking her hand and showing her where the bathroom was and the dressing room that was attached.

"Wow. I think your bathroom is bigger than my bedroom," she said as he set her bag down on the counter.

"It might be," he said with a little laugh. "Wait until you have a shower in the morning."

"I might have to play hooky from work tomorrow, too," she said.

"Well, actually you are playing hooky until tomorrow night. Molly called Colleen this afternoon when I stopped by on my way home. I hope that's okay."

"It's okay, under one condition."

"What's that?"

"You have to stay with me" She smiled.

"I'm way ahead of you, pretty girl. I'm going to clean up in the guest bath across the hall, so take your time. Yell if you need anything," he said, kissing her cheek before closing the door and allowing her some privacy.

She rifled around in her bag and grabbed her toothbrush and face wash. As she set them on the counter, she found two soft towels folded neatly for her. He wanted her to be comfortable in his home. A home that he'd painstakingly renovated with his own two hands, she realized as she ran her fingers over the cool smooth surface of the marble or perhaps granite counter.

She could feel her heart fluttering in her chest as she thought about their night so far. She wondered if he'd just given her space and essentially the power to determine how the rest of the evening went.

When she opened the door, she was certain of it. She heard the familiar jingle of his belt as he started to loosen it and she knew that he wasn't going to push her, so she decided to take matters into her own hand.

"Wait," she whispered, following the sounds of his breathing.

When she felt the solid wall of his chest beneath her hands, she followed the ridge that ran down the middle of his stomach until her hands found the belt buckle and began to loosen its hold. She heard his breath catch as the backs of her fingers grazed his bare skin before she went to work on the buttons. His breath was warm against her cheek as he watched her hands pull the buttons free before letting his pants slide to the ground.

"Pretty girl, we're walking a tight rope here. I want to be good, but right now everything about you is begging me to be very bad," he whispered as his right hand slid underneath the veil of her hair and pulled her in for a scorching kiss. Her skin prickled with heat as his words settled around her and every part of her wanted desperately to feel what he was offering.

"Please. Please be bad," she whispered as she let her teeth graze over the corded muscles of his neck.

As soon as the words left her mouth, Mason lifted her into the air and let her legs wrap around his back before walking over to set her on his bed.

90

"When I'm with you, I feel like my skin is on fire. My heart races like I've never felt before. Can you feel it?" he asked her.

Her hands traveled up to his shoulders as she pressed her lips over his heart. "I can feel everything," she whispered, kissing her way to his lips once more.

"God, I've never been so nervous in my life. What do you do to me?" he asked.

"I love you," she answered simply before climbing the rest of the way into the bed.

When she felt it dip under his weight, she eased back against the pillow, knowing he would follow, and he didn't disappoint. She felt his hands gently brush her hair back from her face.

Mason memorized everything about this moment; the pink tint of her cheeks and the way her lips glistened in the soft light of the candles on the nightstand.

"Mase, stop thinking so hard and do the things that you think you shouldn't. Please," she begged. "I want all of you." She felt the vibration from the groan that fell from his lips and gasped as she finally felt the leash he'd been holding so tightly start snap free.

His hands held hers as he placed them above her head, their fingers tangled together as her body pressed against his in search of any kind of contact. His lips followed the thin strap of her camisole until he reached the soft expanse of skin just below her collarbone.

When his hands began a slow burning path from her fingertips down to her elbows, she could feel his hands start to shake, but when she felt them slide beneath the hem of her camisole, she could no longer tell if the shaking was coming from him or from her. For every inch of skin his fingers exposed, his lips would follow, setting her on fire with each flick of his tongue and he hadn't even really touched her yet.

She knew the second his work-roughened hands scraped over her skin he wouldn't be the only one fighting to remain in control. And she knew once that control was lost that things were going to get explosive.

She wanted that more than she wanted her next breath.

As her back bowed from the bed in search of more, Mason could do nothing but give her what she needed as he lifted her

91

towards his waiting mouth. The moan that tore from her throat only fueled the fire as he pushed back and placed his hands over her hipbones. Seconds later, his tongue lashed over the skin like a warm blade carving through butter, leaving a blistering trail as he eased the silky fabric down her legs.

"So beautiful," he whispered as his hands trailed gently back over her legs until he was able to lift her onto his lap as he sat in front of her. She felt a shudder track through his entire body as he felt the warmth of her bare skin against his for the first time.

They sat like that for what seemed an eternity as he breathed her in, trying desperately to center himself. He'd almost succeeded until he felt her tiny hands begin to push at the last piece of clothing between them, and he was just gone. He was sitting upright one minute as they both pushed and yanked his boxers impatiently from his body; the next she was on her back with his entire weight pressing down around her. His lips dragged the oxygen from her lungs as he kissed her, every muscle vibrating with need.

When there was no air left for them to claim, she felt him pull back and heard the rattle of the drawer beside them. The sound of tearing plastic causing a wave of goose bumps to raise over her skin.

"Please tell me this is what you want," he whispered. Dakota hitched a leg over his hip, pulling him in closer, forcing a frustrated groan to leave his lungs, "Please. Please tell me. Say the words."

"I...want. I need all of you. Everything you have to give. Please, Mason."

A second later, all control flew out the window as Mason laced his fingers with hers and shuddered convulsively as he thrust forward before leaning into another fiery kiss. The slow caress of lips and tongue were in complete contrast to the fingernails scraping across flesh and the unbridled moans that were floating through the air minutes later.

"God, so good," Dakota cried into the air, tearing a guttural groan from Mason's chest.

Mason's hands shook as he lifted her hips off the bed, breaking the coil that nearly sent him spiraling after her as she screamed his name. His movements were no longer controlled, as he was consumed with the need to share in her pleasure.

Sweat dripped down his back while he listened to her breathy moans and felt her fingernails rake over his forearms as they both felt his control slip away.

His whole body shaking from the effort; he shifted their weight so that his back was pressed to the mattress as he tried to hold onto this moment for as long as he possibly could. Pleasure was now pulsing down his spine like jolts of electricity as he clung to the last thin threads of coherency. The second he felt the current pulse through her again, every last ounce of restraint he had chased her name from his lips until she echoed his name on her own waves of release.

Little shocks of pleasure continued to pulse between them as they worked to catch their breath.

"Holy shit. That was...." Mason shuddered, setting off a whole new wave of sparks between them. Dakota ran her fingernails over the ridges of his abdominal muscles, eliciting another groan of satisfaction from his lips and without thought, she found herself pinned beneath his substantial weight as he dragged his teeth across her collarbone.

"Do that again and we're going to see just how much stamina I have," he whispered.

She smiled as she told him, "I knew I wanted to do more than just lick the frosting."

"Wait a minute, what?" Mason asked as he thought about that statement.

"Cupcake," she whispered as the blush quickly rose on her cheeks.

"Huh? Oh! That's what had you all flustered," he said as he kissed her once more.

"The other day when you left the diner, Molly said you looked at me like you wanted to lick the frosting off the cupcake."

"Dakota, I'll lick anything you want me to," he whispered as he watched desire bloom across her cheeks and chest. "Wait, and you told her you wanted to do more than lick the frosting?"

"I didn't mean to tell her that; it just kind of slipped out." She laughed.

"So what was that about today?"

"Molly decided to torture me and tell Melinda."

"Oh, well, that should give her something to share with my brother, who will undoubtedly bring it up repeatedly." He laughed.

"If it's any consolation, I meant every word and I intend to follow through on it very soon," she finished in a more sultry tone.

"Tomorrow's not going to suck then," he said with a laugh.

"It will if you ask nicely," she told him as his laughter turned into more of a whimper.

"I'll be right back. Do you want some water?" he asked as he wandered into the bathroom.

"Yes, please."

Once they'd had their fill of water, he pulled the covers up and whispered, "Best day ever." Before he quickly stole one last kiss and pulled her into his arms.

Sleep came quickly as exhaustion finally took over.

Chapter 10

Mason woke up around seven the next morning and stretched as he pulled Dakota into his arms. The temperature rose several degrees as he let one hand travel the length of her spine, settling against her thigh. He used the other to thread his fingers through the hair at the nape of her neck, letting her draw the air from his lungs as she kissed her way from the stubble on his jaw to the dip between his muscled chest and the sharp ridge of his abs.

"Dakota. What are you doing to me?"

"I'd imagine about the same thing that you do to me," she whispered as she traced the hard planes of his stomach until she reached the sharp V where his abs met his hipbones. Mason's skin felt alive as her fingertips mapped out every ridge and scar along the way until they were ghosting over his happy trail, eliciting a deep groan.

Seconds later, he felt her breath ruffle the soft line of hair that started just below his navel, following it down until she found what she'd been after. Mason's head fell back as his entire body bowed with the pleasure her lips and tongue sent coursing through every nerve ending in his body.

His hands gently threaded into her hair as he did all he could not to give in to the charge that was firing down his spine, until a little moan left her throat sending vibrations coursing through his body and destroying his resolve.

"Dakota, please God. You have to slow down," he moaned.

He could feel her shake ever so gently as she laughed with her refusal to do as he asked.

"Oh fuck!" he bellowed as he knew he was about to lose the battle over his already shaky control. His fingers tightened slightly in her hair as he tried once more to dissuade her, but she was determined. Her name fell from his lips as he threw his head back and squeezed his eyes shut while he simply enjoyed the sensations that were coursing through his body.

As the ringing in his ears began to dissipate, he felt her shake with laughter.

"You know most men, myself included, do not typically like to hear a woman laugh after she goes down on him," he whispered, feeling just a bit self-conscious.

"I'm not laughing at you; I'm laughing because I'll never be able to enjoy a cupcake without turning a ridiculous shade of pink ever again."

Mason laughed as he thought about the beautiful flush that covered her skin when she shared her comment the night before.

"I think I might enjoy that flush, knowing what you'll be thinking about. I'll be thinking about it, too," he whispered as he eased her back against the pillows, allowing his lips to blaze a trail from her earlobe to the soft column of her throat on his way to returning the favor, until they both heard a frantic pounding and ringing coming from Mason's front door.

Without even thinking, Mason pulled on a pair of shorts and handed his t-shirt to Dakota before he picked up his gun and said, "Stay here. I'm sure Dev just locked himself out or something."

"Okay," she answered as she listened to him quietly unlock the bedroom door and move down the hallway.

As soon as he got to the first floor, she heard him say, "Melinda! What the hell? Your ass better be on fire or something!"

"No, but Dakota's house is," she said quietly, sounding out of breath.

"What! When the hell did that happen?"

"About twenty minutes ago, I was on my way here when the call went out. There was an explosion or something."

Mason turned for the stairs and raced back to his bedroom, hoping that Dakota had dressed in his absence, as he was certain to have three cops on his heels.

"Dakota?" Mason said as he approached the door, but his hesitation died as he heard the sound of her phone ringing.

"I've got it," he said as he grabbed the phone, waving off the rest of the team for the moment.

"This is Mason."

"Oh, thank God!" Molly wailed into the phone. "She's with you?"

"Yes, she's here and she's fine. I'll have her call you in a minute, okay?"

"Thank you," Molly whispered as she hung up the phone.

"What's going on, Mason?"

"Dakota, that was Molly. She was calling to check on you," Mason started.

"Oh for God's sake; she was calling to get details already!" Dakota laughed. "Couldn't she at least let me enjoy my morning off?"

"I'm sure that she would have, but it seems there was an incident at your house. Molly was concerned about you."

"What happened? Did someone break in? I know there have been a few break-ins in the area," she asked, moderately concerned.

Mason took a deep breath, knowing the calm was about to vanish. "No, love. There was an explosion."

His heart ached as he watched horror wash over her face. Her hand shook as she covered her mouth and tears clung to her lashes. Mason climbed onto the bed beside her and wrapped his arms around her.

"Is everything gone?" she whispered.

Devon walked into the room with a glass of water and prepared to share the information they'd been able to get while they were talking.

"Dakota, it seems there was an explosion in the basement. So far, they don't know what caused it, but there is going to be a full investigation. Melinda and Piper just left. They're going to meet with the investigator and see what they can find out. And I spoke to Judy. She and Molly and Colleen are going to stop by in an hour or so."

"Oh God, it's gone? My house is gone?" she asked.

"I'm so sorry, Dakota," Devon said as he placed the glass of water in her hand and sat in the chair across the room.

"What if I'd gone home last night? What if we'd both been there?" she whispered.

"Thank God you didn't, both of you. I'm not prepared to lose either one of you," Devon answered quietly, clearly shaken by that possibility.

As she thought about the "what ifs," she felt Mason's warm hands brush against her cheeks before he said, "You are welcome here; you know that. We'll get you whatever you need."

He wrapped his arms around her just as her shoulders began to shake violently as she felt the crushing loss of everything that gave her comfort. The last pieces of her memories with her mother, the safety and comfort of a place she knew so well. All of it was gone. Mason pulled out his phone and texted Melinda as he rubbed a hand over her back and whispered, "I've got you."

Melinda and Piper had just pulled up to the house when Mason's text came through. He'd asked Melinda how bad it was and if there was anything to salvage. Her heart sank as she looked at the mess of water, black smoke, and steam rippling off what remained of Dakota's house as it mixed with the chill in the air, knowing that her response would probably be "no."

She looked around at the crowds of people gawking at debris, scanning their expressions as an uneasy feeling crept over her.

The fire inspector, Andrew Davies, interrupted her thoughts as he made his way over to speak with them. He'd known the Cole brothers since pre-school, so Melinda and Piper's arrival got his attention.

"Hey, Melinda, Piper. What brings Serial Crimes to a fire?"

"The home belonged to Mase's girlfriend, Dakota Shelton," Melinda answered.

"Oh. Well, fortunately no one was in the residence when the explosion occurred."

"We know that. She was with Mason, thank God," Piper said. "Was it intentional?"

"I won't know for sure until we do a full investigation."

"Off the record. What does your gut say?" Melinda asked.

"Yes, I think it was intentional. When we arrived on the scene, the fire was burning way too hot for a typical house fire and there was a distinct chemical odor. Also, it would appear that a couple of the windows on the upper floor had been broken from the outside before the explosion."

"How can you tell that?' Piper asked.

"Because the windows on the main level blew out after we arrived. The fire moved up from the basement, so it's unlikely they blew out before the lower level and there wasn't enough glass on the ground to suggest they'd been broken from inside. It looks like they were broken to vent the fire so it would spread up faster."

"Inspector Davies, did you or any of your men find anything....unusual when you arrived?" Melinda asked.

"You mean aside from the obviously broken windows?"

"Yes. Like any people that appeared to be interested in the fire, or anything that might have looked out of place?"

"You think this is a part of that Reaper case, don't you?" Davies whispered as he looked around.

"We don't have any reason to believe Dakota would be a target, but we can't ignore the fact that another woman close to Mase might have been targeted," Piper shared.

"Oh crap. This is related to Jill, isn't it?" Davies asked.

Neither Piper nor Melinda answered, but Davies had been close enough to Mason to know their silence was as good as a confirmation.

"I'll send all of our findings to your people as soon as we're done with it," Davies said before he turned back to his men. "Tell Mason that I'm sorry and that I'll come by when we have some answers."

"Will do," Piper answered.

Piper started to head back to the car, but Melinda wasn't in front of him anymore. So he turned back and scanned the surrounding area until he caught sight of her red jacket rounding the corner. "Hey, Mel! What are you doing?" he yelled.

As he turned the corner, he slammed into her back. She was standing over a scattered pile of white roses in the alley across from Dakota's house. "Get the camera," she said.

Piper ran to the car and pulled the camera from the backseat, then jogged back to where Melinda stood staring at the ominous signature that let them know Dakota was now a target.

Piper snapped pictures of the roses and anything nearby that could be evidence before he placed the roses into a bag to take to the lab. He called it in and had their forensic team come out to make sure anything else that could possibly be related was collected, but an alley in the city was a pretty broad canvas in terms of what was possibly evidence and what was trash.

Melinda called the lab and made sure that both Andy and Robin were in to deal with the evidence that was headed their way from the alley as well as anything the fire department was able to turn up before they made their way back to Mason's house.

Piper sat in the car while Melinda ran into Target and grabbed some toiletries and a few changes of clothes for Dakota, knowing that she had lost everything except for what she had with her at Mason's the night before. It wasn't much, but it was the best she could offer for the moment.

Mason stared at Devon and ran his fingers through Dakota's hair while she clung to his side. They both knew this was more than an accident, and Mason's gut turned as he thought about this guy getting close enough to take anyone else that he cared about. He knew that he'd been lucky to survive such a loss the first time, and he wasn't about to let him have another chance.

After about a half an hour, Mason's doorbell rang and Devon made his way down to answer it. He knew the instant they hit the first flight of stairs that Molly, Colleen, and Judy were on their way up as the sound of their concerned voices echoed from below.

A light knock sounded on the door, then Mason said, "Come in."

When the three women laid eyes on Dakota, all of them burst into tears.

"We'll be in the kitchen if you need us," Mason said as he kissed her forehead. "I'm just going to put some coffee on. Shout if you need anything."

Devon was pacing in the kitchen when Mason walked in. "I don't want to make a bad day worse, but you need to see this."

"What?" Mason asked.

Devon handed him his phone with a photo of the roses that Melinda had found.

"I knew it."

"Yeah, well I think we can officially assume Dakota's on his list. So, do you think she's on that list because of you, or was she there all along?"

"I don't know. It seems like too much of a coincidence. It has to be to get at me, right?"

"Then do you think it was about you all along?"

"I don't know? Maybe? But wouldn't I have seen the connection by now? I mean if it's me, then he's killing a bunch of people who aren't connected, because I sure don't know anyone aside from Jill and Dakota. The way he's racking up bodies, it seems like I would have a connection to someone else if I'm the catalyst unless he's just pissed that I am working the case."

"I don't know, but I think we need to talk to Dakota about the case and see if she can make a connection. I know this is the last thing you want to put on her right now, but if there is a connection, she could be the key to finding this asshole."

As if on cue, Dakota came down the stairs with the Judy at her side and the two younger women right behind them.

"What do I need to know?" she asked as she reached out her hand, following Mason's voice. Mason took her hand, leading her to a seat at the bar and sat beside her.

"This wasn't an accident, so we need to know if you were targeted because of me or if you are somehow linked to this case."

"Oh," she said as she sat up a little straighter. "You think this was the Reaper?"

Devon looked up as he realized she knew more than he thought. Obviously, it had been all over the news lately, but he wasn't sure until then that she knew the Reaper was the case they'd been working.

"I do, and I'm so sorry that I put you in danger. I should have stayed away from you," he whispered against her neck as the realization shook through him.

"You don't know that this is your fault. And even if I was targeted because I know you, it's not something that you did. This rests solely on the shoulders of the man responsible. You can't take the blame for that," she told him.

101

Devon poured coffee for her friends as they moved into the living room, leaving Mason and Devon to talk with Dakota.

"I need to ask you some questions about the case. I don't expect that you'll have all the answers, but humor me. How about we start with what you do know?" Mason said.

"Okay."

"You were raised by your aunt and uncle after your parents died, right?"

"Yes."

"Did they legally adopt you?"

"No. My mother named them as my legal guardians in her will. They never adopted me. I don't understand how this is important."

"It may not be, but maybe something will stand out that I'm not connecting. So far, most of the victims have been adopted except for Jill and the last two, though a brother and half sister raised the younger victim after their parents' death. It's unlikely that you were targeted for any other reason than keeping company with his least favorite person, but if there is another connection, it might help us figure out what this guy is after and maybe even who else he's targeting and why."

"Huh. So, apart from Jill, they're all adopted or orphaned," Dakota said as she mulled over the information.

"Yes, what are you thinking?" Devon asked.

"Well, I don't know, but maybe they were in foster homes?" she asked. "I mean, probably not all together, but if they were in the system it's kind of like six degrees of separation. If you spend enough time in there, you cross a lot of the same paths."

"You weren't in the system, were you?" Devon asked, a little confused by her knowledge.

"No, but my aunt and uncle fostered several kids. Some of the kids that got passed around a lot could be pretty volatile and they all had stories that followed them. My uncle liked to take the tough cases because the reimbursement rates were a tiny bit higher. He was a Class A piece of shit, though. I did the best I could to stay away from him because my blindness was a source of entertainment for him and some of the kids they fostered. My aunt was marginally better. She simply thought I was useless because I couldn't see, but she was more smothering than mean."

Mason ran his hand through her hair as she spoke, wanting to destroy the man for the pain that these memories held for Dakota. Devon stood and went to check if anyone needed a refill on coffee, giving the two of them some privacy as he saw Mason's protective instincts begin to claw to the surface. He knew that the conversation was about to take on a more personal tone.

"Did he hurt you?" he asked quietly.

"Sometimes. Mostly, he would just go out of his way to make my day-to-day life difficult. He'd leave things where I could trip on them or move things from their usual place so I couldn't find them easily. He didn't really do anything bad until I was older, maybe fifteen or sixteen. Whenever I stopped being a gangly kid, that's when I figured out that he had taken on a more predatory appreciation. Then, he would wait silently in my bedroom when I got home from school or work."

Mason felt as though he might crack his teeth as he thought about what her uncle had been planning while he waited for her, and worse, watched her.

"He didn't..." Mason started, but he couldn't finish the thought so he just put his hand on her cheek and laid his forehead against hers as he tried to control his rage.

"No, Mase. It wasn't for lack of trying, but he never succeeded. The alcohol usually hindered his ability to follow through, and he liked to see me fight him, I think," she said quietly as she felt his relief and his rage. Most of all, she felt his warmth as he pulled her into his lap and breathed her in, assuring himself that she was right there with him in that moment.

"Is he still living?" Mason asked through his carefully controlled rage.

"Yes."

"Nearby?"

"South Side."

"Does he stop by the diner ever?"

"Sometimes."

Mason kissed her forehead and whispered, "I'll be right back."

After he left the room, Devon came in and refilled her coffee. He told her that Melinda had stopped to get her a few things. She tried to listen for Mason, but she couldn't tell where he'd gone.

In the living room, Mason walked over to Judy and asked her for a minute of her time. He led her onto the balcony and closed the door to ensure some privacy.

"Do you know Dakota's uncle?"

"Yes, of course. We all do our best to run interference when he comes in. He's a real slimy bastard."

"Can you do me a favor and call me the next time he comes in? Make sure that everyone has my number. I'd love to have a chat with him. I'll tell Dakota to do the same, but it would be good if he stayed away from her altogether."

"I really hope he comes by again soon. It'd serve him right to have to deal with a real man instead of picking on Dakota," Judy said with a smile as she kissed his cheek. "I knew you were one of the good ones the first time you sat down in my section."

"Yeah, I figured you'd vetted me long before you let Dakota anywhere near me. I'm glad I passed the test." He smiled.

"Sweetheart, after the second time you showed up at the diner in the middle of the night, I knew you needed her as much as she needs you. Her uncle did a number on her, and I can see that you have some things that haunt you, too. You both deserve the happiness that you have found together. And I can't tell you how happy we all are to have you and your brother looking out for her now, too."

"That's good, because you're all stuck with us now." He smiled as he led her back inside.

Judy sat back down with a smile as she heard Mason tell Dakota that he loved her before he wrapped his arms around her shoulders and kissed the top of her head. When she saw the smile that Dakota gave him and the one he wore in return, she knew that he would do everything in his power to protect the girl that she'd grown to love as much as her own daughter.

Chapter 11

When Piper and Melinda returned, Mason took the bags upstairs to his room and set them on his bed.

Devon came up after a few minutes to let him know that Judy and Colleen were making some lunch.

They were silent for a minute before Devon said, "I got a little more info on the uncle from Molly while you were talking to Dakota earlier."

"Oh, yeah."

"Yup. Name, address, workplace, all the important details in case you wanted to pay him a visit. I'd be happy to tag along."

"Seems he likes to visit her. So I asked Judy to make sure they call me."

"Yeah, I gave Molly all of our numbers, too. Told her to call any of us if he pays her a visit. Great minds, Mase," he said with a smile.

"Is that the only reason you gave Molly your number?" Mason asked.

"I don't know. I might be hoping she'll call me sometime." He laughed. His laughter stopped as another thought occurred to him. "Do you think her uncle could be the Reaper?"

"He might be a little old for the profile, but I certainly wouldn't rule it out until we sift through the foster care connection and have a chat with him. He sounds like a real prize."

"Did you get a chance to ask her about any of the victims? Did she recognize any of the names?"

"No. I got a little side tracked by her uncle and a desire to return the favors he bestowed on Dakota."

"Understandable. I wasn't in the room and I was finding it hard not to focus on the same thing. Please tell me that he didn't do anything that would warrant actions that require an alibi and maybe a shovel," Devon said quietly.

"No. Though I can't make any promises on the alibi. She said he found the struggle more enjoyable and that the alcohol hindered his ability to follow through on the thoughts he seemed to be entertaining, a very small consolation, but I'd still like to remove an appendage for entertaining those thoughts," Mason answered.

"Noted. Maybe we should go back downstairs before we get too far into plotting suitable punishments. We can get back to the questions after everyone else gets back to the diner," Devon said.

"Yeah. I'm not looking forward to going through the case details with her, but hopefully it will give us something else to go on."

When they entered the kitchen, there was a lot of chatter as everyone had made themselves at home. Judy had a large pot on the stove and Colleen was peeling the skin off of some tomatillos and roasted jalapenos. Suddenly, he realized his house felt like a home with all of his friends and the woman that had simultaneously stolen and mended his heart.

All the people that he cared about were gathered around the island as he walked up behind Dakota and whispered in her ear, "I love this. You, and our friends together. It feels like family."

"Me, too," she whispered as she leaned into his embrace.

After they all sat down and enjoyed warm bowls of posole verde, Judy, Colleen, and Molly went back to the diner. They'd closed earlier in the day for a "family emergency," but they knew they needed to get the doors open for their regular dinner crowd.

There were now two unmarked cars stationed in front and behind the diner twenty-four/seven, as well as two uniforms inside at all times. On that, Mason wouldn't budge. A line had been crossed when they weren't looking and he wasn't about to let him take anything or anyone else from Dakota.

Dakota sat on the couch with Mason at her side and Devon in the chair beside them.

"So what can I help you with? Do you think the killer has some kind of connection to me or what?" Dakota asked.

"We don't know what the connection is, but I was thinking maybe we could start with the victims. See if any names ring a bell from the kids fostered by your aunt and uncle."

"Okay. That sounds good. I don't remember all of them, but hopefully their names will ring a bell," Dakota said. They all knew she was at a disadvantage since descriptions meant nothing and it wasn't like she could hear their voices for recognition.

"Well, let's start with Jill Stroh. That was his first victim that we know of," Mason said.

"Your girlfriend?" she asked, although she already knew the answer.

"Yes."

"No. Was she in the system?"

"No. Her dad died when she was young. We don't know anything about her mother, but I don't think Jill had any contact with her after she graduated and went off to college."

"So, unless she happened to come into the diner, it's unlikely that we had any connection that's relevant."

"Julianne Howard," Devon offered next.

"Nope. We had mostly boys," Dakota told them.

"Jonathon Beauford."

"Baby Jon. I remember we had a little boy named Jon. I think his last name may have been Morrow, or Monroe maybe. I know it started with an M. He wasn't with us long before he was adopted. I don't know if it's the same boy, but I recall him having horrible nightmares."

"Nightmares?" Mason asked, recalling the conversation with Mr. and Mrs. Beauford.

"Yes. About roses, I think. He was maybe around three so he didn't talk much, but they were always about roses."

She felt Mason's breath a moment before he kissed her cheek. "I think you just gave us our first break!"

Dakota smiled at him as he jumped up and headed to the kitchen to share the info with Piper and Melinda to see if they could confirm a child named Jonathon Morrow or Monroe and link him back to the Beaufords, I think Jon Beauford was fostered with Dakota's aunt and uncle briefly. Then he grabbed his cell phone and called Mr. Beauford's cell.

"Good afternoon, Mr. Beauford, This is Lt. Commander Mason Cole. I was wondering if I might be able to sit down with you and your wife for a few minutes today."

"Sure. We were just going to go down to the lounge for a cup of coffee. Would you like us to meet you at the station?"

"No, sir, I can come to you. I don't want to disrupt your afternoon too much. I just have a few follow-up questions for you. I'll be by in about an hour," Mason said.

"Okay. We'll see you then," Mr. Beauford said, and ended the call.

When Mason returned to the living room, he shared the conversation with Devon and Dakota.

"So, are we heading over there now?"

"Yes. Dakota, are you okay with Piper and Melinda?"

"Would it be okay if I came with you? I need to get out of the house for a bit."

"Dakota and I can take a walk or something while you talk to the Beaufords," Devon offered.

"Sure. Then we can grab some dinner on the way home."

"I just need to grab a sweater." Dakota said as she stood, but then she sat down as she realized all the things she didn't have now.

"Dakota, Melinda brought you some clothes for the next couple of days. We can go out tomorrow and get whatever else you need," Mason said, taking her hand and leading her up to his room to go through the bags.

"Thank you," she whispered. "For letting me stay here."

"Dakota, waking up with you in my arms made me feel whole for the first time in a long time. My house feels like a home with you in it, so I'll do anything I can to make you feel comfortable here," Mason said as he kissed her forehead.

"You make me feel comfortable. As long as you're here, this is home," she said, wrapping her arms around his waist.

"I'm not going anywhere, love," he said, leaning down and kissing her softly as he threaded his hands through her hair.

Mason helped her find a sweater and they headed back downstairs to meet Devon and head to the Marriott, where the Beaufords were staying.

Thirty minutes later, Devon and Dakota sat down at a table in the corner of the Marriott Hotel lounge, while Mason sat on the other side of the room with Jonathon Beauford's parents.

Mrs. Beauford had smiled as Mason kissed Dakota on the cheek before heading over to their table.

"Is that your girlfriend?" Mrs. Beauford asked.

"Yes, it is," Mason told her with a smile.

"She's very pretty."

"Thank you. She's actually part of the reason I called to see you," he told the couple.

"Oh?"

"I remembered you mentioning that Jonathon had nightmares when he came to you, about roses, right?"

"Yes, every night, and it broke our hearts," Mrs. Beauford stated.

"Do you by chance know what his last name was before you adopted him? I'm not sure how that works with older children."

"He was about three years old when we got him. So we knew his last name, but we didn't know much about where he came from. He had been in foster care prior to that. His last name was Morrow. Did your young lady know our boy? Is that why you called us here?" Mr. Beauford said.

"I believe that she might have been in the foster home with him," he said.

"Oh, please, can we talk to her?" Mrs. Beauford asked.

"Sure. Let me just go get her," Mason said as he stood and walked over to the table Devon and Dakota were seated at.

Mrs. Beauford smiled as she saw Mason take Dakota's hand and guide it to his elbow. She watched as they walked back, her hand on his elbow and Mason whispering in her ear as they slowly made their way through the lounge. The room was bustling by now and she couldn't help but notice the look of discomfort on the young woman's face. When a man turned from the bar and nearly toppled the woman, she noticed Mason put an arm out to stop his forward momentum before pulling her into his arms and whispering once again.

When they arrived at the table, she watched Mason pull out her chair and help her get situated.

"Mr. and Mrs. Beauford, you remember my brother Devon. And this is my girlfriend, Dakota Shelton," Mason said when they were all seated.

Tears filled the woman's eyes as Mason introduced them.

"Hello, dear. I'm Helene and this is my husband, Gene," she said as she looked between Mason and Dakota. "Pardon me for being so forward, but how long have you been blind?"

"Since I was four. It's not a big deal normally. I just don't like crowds," Dakota said with a smile.

"I can't say I'm a big fan myself and I can see the obstacles," Mrs. Beauford told her.

"Well, it's very nice to meet both of you." Dakota smiled. "I am so sorry for your loss. Mason told me Jon's last name was Morrow and about the nightmares. I think he lived with us for a few months before you adopted him."

"He had the nightmares when he lived with you?" Mr. Beauford asked.

"He did. About roses. I never understood what they were about, but they terrified him. I used to sit with him for hours in a rocking chair trying to get him calmed down. I always wondered about where he went. He was such a sweet little boy."

"Yes, he was. I never knew what it meant, but when I used to rock him back to sleep, he used to say a word that I never understood until now. He used to cry and say 'Kota' over and over. Now I understand. He was talking about you," Mrs. Beauford said. "Thank you for being good to our boy."

"I should thank you," Dakota said. "You gave him a home and family."

"Were you adopted eventually?" Mr. Beauford asked.

"No, I was living with my aunt and uncle after my parents passed away. They had a number of fosters."

"Oh, I'm sorry, honey. At least you had family," Mrs. Beauford said.

When Dakota didn't say anything, Mrs. Beauford seemed to understand. "They weren't good to you?"

"My aunt was fine, maybe a little smothering," Dakota answered.

"But your uncle, he wasn't fine, was he?"

110

"No, ma'am. That's why I would take care of Jon. He wasn't a patient man. I was sad to see Jon go, but I was relieved because I didn't want him to be a target like I was."

"Well, dear, it looks like you've done just fine for yourself. This young man is quite smitten with you, I can tell," Mrs. Beauford said as she pat her hand.

"That feeling is mutual. He's a good man."

"She owns a diner, and she's quite a chef, too," Mason said with pride.

"That's rather impressive," Mr. Beauford added.

"Thank you. I love it, and that's how I met Mason." Dakota smiled.

"We'll have to stop by while we're in town. I can't thank you enough dear for talking to us about our boy. It's quite nice to remember how he came into our lives. Speaking of, Lt. Commander Cole, I thought of something else that might help you. There was a caseworker; I know his first name was Peter and he worked out of an office on Montrose near Lake Shore Drive. That's where we picked up our boy. Maybe he can give you more information on where Jonathon came from," Mrs. Beauford shared.

"You can call me 'Mason.' That's very helpful Mrs. Beauford. Thank you."

"I hope that it helps you find out what happened to our son and stop anyone else from losing their child."

"I will stop this man," Mason said with conviction.

Mrs. Beauford watched as Mason looked at Dakota and she thought she saw fear in his eyes as he pulled the young woman closer to him.

"He's after her, isn't he?" Mrs. Beauford surmised.

A look of shock came across the brothers' faces before Devon said, "Yes. She seems to be in his crosshairs. When he made it clear that she was a target, we started to question his link to her, so when we mentioned the adoption link, she suggested looking into foster care, too. We think the man responsible may have been in foster care himself. We know there is a possibility that he's after her to get to Mason, but we have to look at the possibility that there might be a deeper link than that. The

111

connection with your son might be the first break we have and it makes it look like the foster care link is what ties it all together."

"Why would he single you out? I don't understand," Mr. Beauford said.

"I honestly don't know, but do you remember the photograph I showed you when you were at the precinct?" Mason asked.

"Yes. Your girlfriend, right?"

"Yes. We know now that she was most likely one of his first victims. He wanted me on this case; he wanted me to know he was back," Mason said. "I don't think he knew who I was back then, but I was on a mission after she died. I wanted vengeance, so I took this job and swore I would find the man responsible. In doing that, I think I fed his thirst. I marked myself as his ultimate adversary, his end game. He knows that I won't stop until he's behind bars or dead, and I'm thinking he's hoping for death."

"I think that's why you're the best person for this case. I don't mean to diminish how much this man has taken from you, but it gives me comfort to know that you know our pain, our loss. I know that your loss will drive you to find this man, and that makes all of this just a little less hopeless," Mr. Beauford said.

"I will find him. I promise you," Mason said as he pulled Dakota into his side.

"I know you will," Mr. Beauford said, standing and helping his wife from her seat. "We'll stay in town for a few more days unless you need us to stay longer."

"I'll let you know. I appreciate you talking to us."

"We appreciate your candor. I know it's probably more than you would normally share. Dakota, it was lovely to meet you and thank you for sharing the connection you had to our son," Mr. Beauford said.

"Keep her safe," Mrs. Beauford whispered in his ear, and then she hugged Dakota.

"Have a good night," Mason said to the couple.

They all said their goodbyes as they left the lounge. Mason, Devon, and Dakota headed back to the house.

Chapter 12

Before the three of them had made their way home, Mason's phone vibrated with a text message from an unknown caller.

The message contained a single photograph of a blonde woman who looked to be in her mid-fifties. She was standing at train stop, but the location was unclear. Beneath the picture read, "Say goodbye to her mother."

Mason looked at the screen as he tried to figure out what the message meant. Whose mother was she? Should he know her?

"You going to share with the rest of the class or just stare a hole through the thing?" Devon asked.

"I don't understand. Who is this and why is she important? She's too old to be linked through foster care, unless she was one of the foster parents, but why this one and not others if she is?" Mason thought aloud.

Mason forwarded the text to Melinda and asked that she try and trace the phone it came from as well as isolate the background and see if they could figure out where it was taken and possibly when.

Twenty minutes later, Mason's phone rang.

"Hey, Melinda, what have you got?" he asked as he placed her on speaker.

"Well, we were able to get a closer look at a city sticker in one of the car windows in the background. Based on that, I'd say it was the Winnetka Metra stop. There was also a newspaper rack and the paper was from today. With the shadows and the number of people present at peak hours, I think the picture may have been taken not too long before it was sent to you."

"Dev, let's get Dakota to the diner. Melinda, get units to the Metra station ASAP! We're on our way to Winnetka. I'll get in touch when we're closer," Mason said before disconnecting the call.

Devon flipped on the lights and sirens and flew to the diner, where Mason saw Dakota inside. He made sure the officers were aware that she was in the building before he left. From there, they headed straight for the Winnetka station, arriving in less than a half an hour, but they both knew it was unlikely that she or the Reaper would still be there.

When they arrived, the potential witnesses were being shuttled back to the local precinct for questioning. Melinda had texted him to let him know that she and Piper would be waiting there to question them.

Mason saw the officer that appeared to be in charge of the scene and quickly jogged in his direction.

"I'm Lt. Commander Mason Cole with Serial Crimes. This is Detective Devon Cole. Sorry for creating such a stir, but we have reason to believe that a material witness in our case was here. Did you see this woman when you arrived?" Mason asked as he held up his phone to show the officer the picture he'd received.

"No, I don't recognize her. You are more than welcome to check the bus, maybe someone saw her, if nothing else," the officer said.

Mason walked down the aisle of the bus until he found an older woman that recognized her.

"That's Angela Forrester. She takes the 4:35 towards Kenosha every Friday, though I'm not sure where she gets off. I saw her earlier; she should be on the bus with us," the woman said, looking around and suddenly becoming a little distraught.

"How do you know Ms. Forrester?"

"She buys flowers from my shop every Friday for her daughter. I have a little kiosk in the station. Always white roses and never a card. She always looks so sad. This picture; it's from today? She was wearing the same sweater."

"I think so, yes. Do you know where I can find her daughter, perhaps?"

"No, I'm afraid I don't."

"Well, thank you. You've been very helpful," Mason told her before he exited the bus, tapping the side to indicate that the driver was free to take them back to the station, then he made his way back to Devon.

"Well, we've officially found the driver of the second vehicle that killed Mr. and Mrs. Hartrey. She buys white roses for her daughter every Friday from a kiosk before taking the Kenosha line. I don't want to draw a conclusion about the roses since they are probably one of the most common flowers one might purchase, but every Friday seems more like a memorial than a gift. Maybe she goes to a cemetery wherever her destination is?" Mason wondered.

"Always goes back to that, huh? You know that there have to be hundreds of cemeteries between here and the end of the line, right, Mase?" Devon said.

"I know. There has to be something else here. No way did this guy all of a sudden get cagey on the details. He likes to leave breadcrumbs everywhere he's been."

"Maybe we should check the kiosk?" Devon offered.

Mason continued to think aloud as they searched for clues, "So, if he somehow blames this woman, why not just kill her? Why kill the others? To get to her, maybe? But then why even threaten Dakota? If she's the end game, why not just kill her and go back into hiding?" Mason rambled.

"Good questions, all of them, but I don't think we're going to be able to fully piece this together until he's sitting in front of us and I'm not sure that he intends to stay breathing for that encounter, particularly if Dakota is his end game. You and I both know he won't survive going after her, no matter what the outcome," Devon answered.

Mason didn't respond to that assessment, but Devon could see the tension in his jaw as he considered all the possible outcomes.

They found nothing in the area surrounding the kiosk, so after about an hour of searching they decided it was time to head back to the city and check in with the team, and Mason was itching to get eyes on Dakota again. Not being with her was making him very uneasy, now that they knew she was targeted. The conversation with his brother didn't seem to help him either. He followed Devon back to the car, but stopped abruptly as he noticed an envelope stuck under the windshield wiper.

"So help me, if I got a ticket...." Devon started to say as Mason grabbed his hand and shook his head to stop. Devon looked at his brother as he realized it wasn't a ticket at all.

Mason reached into his coat pocket and pulled out a pair of gloves before he reached over and pulled the envelope free. He carefully pulled the flap on the envelope and slid the message out.

Once again, the note had been written in a rusty brown scrawl that Mason was certain had once resided in the veins of one of the victims, or perhaps his latest victim. This did not bode well for Ms. Forrester.

Find your way back to her, and you'll find your way back to me.

Mason looked around, but he was certain the Reaper was long gone. There was no way to know for sure that he'd been the one to leave the message, for that matter. They would have to hope that the surveillance cameras in and around the Metra station could give them a visual on whoever left the note, where Angela Forrester got off to and if she'd been alone.

"Who are we finding our way back to? Angela Forrester? Or someone else?" Mason asked.

"I don't know, but hopefully something about Angela Forrester will help us figure out who we're dealing with, because this cloak and dagger bullshit is really starting to piss me off," Devon answered.

The pair rode in silence until Devon broke into his distracted thoughts. "You going to go in, or should I?"

Mason looked up and saw that he had parked in front of the diner, so he stepped out of the car and headed in to get Dakota.

"Hi, Judy. How's everybody doing?" he asked as he looked for Dakota.

"She's in the back. We're all a little shaken up, but we're doing fine. Six cops on the place at all times seems a bit excessive though, hon."

"Maybe it is, but I'm not going to let him take anyone or anything else from her."

"I understand, but who's going to look out for you? She's not going to say anything, but I know she's afraid for you," Judy told him.

"I know. I've got Dev with me, and we have cops on my place, too. I don't think he wants me, though. I'm the mouse he tortures, not the one he kills. I'm more worried about the people I care about. And that includes all of you."

"Go back and see Miss Dakota. She's been on the verge of tears ever since you left a few hours ago. She needs you."

Mason walked into the back, checking the kitchen. Molly looked up and smiled before pointing a flour-covered hand towards the closed office door.

Mason knocked gently. When he didn't get a response, he opened the door and found Dakota sitting on the couch with her arms wrapped tightly around her legs. He could hear the music from her iPod and he could see the tears that clung to her cheeks.

He walked over to stand in front of her as he reached out and gently brushed a tear from her cheek while he carefully pulled the ear buds free. She held her breath as she waited for him to say something even though her heart already knew it was him.

"Dakota?" he whispered.

The second she heard his voice, she launched herself into his arms and let everything she'd been holding go. Mason sat back on the couch she'd vacated and rubbed her back as she cried. He knew that it was what she needed, but it tore him apart anyway.

She never said a word, so he just held her until she went limp in his arms. He knew that her whole world had been turned upside down in less than a twenty-four hour period. It would have been a lot for anyone to process, but for Dakota it had been a much deeper burden.

After a few minutes, Mason stood with Dakota in his arms. He grabbed her coat and draped it over her as best he could before walking out into the dining room.

"Would you mind grabbing the door?" Mason asked Judy.

The older woman stepped up and tucked Dakota's coat around her a bit more securely before grabbing the door and helping Mason get her into the car. When she was settled, Mason slid in beside her and pulled her back into his arms once more.

"I take it she's having a tougher time with all this than she let on earlier?" Devon asked.

"I think so. Can't say that I blame her."

"Melinda and Piper are waiting at the house. I'll fill them in on what we found and see what they learned from the witnesses.

Take some time; we can hash it all out in a few hours," Devon said as he pulled into the garage behind Mason's place.

Devon opened the door for Mason, waving to Melinda and Piper to be quiet. They watched as he dropped her coat in the doorway and headed up the stairs before either of them spoke.

"I'm not sure which one of them looks more destroyed," Piper said.

"I know. I can't even imagine what losing her house must be like. He took the one place she felt confident and in control from her. The one space that never changed. I know she feels comfortable at the diner, but it doesn't have the same predictability as her home did," Devon said as he glanced over Melinda's shoulder.

After a minute, Melinda shifted a post-it note in his direction, "So I looked into any place that this man Peter may have worked at on Montrose. Turns out, Children's Services has an office up that way. I spoke to one of the caseworkers and he told me that there's a man named Peter Donahue that worked there for over twenty years. Apparently, he's semi-retired after an accident, but he still works from home on the few of his cases that are still active."

Melinda pointed to the screen as she played the footage that she'd been looking at for Devon.

"We have Angela Forrester on the surveillance feed talking to someone who is just out of frame on the platform, but then she turns abruptly to go inside and he or she doesn't seem follow. After that, she turns up in the parking lot looking like she's on the run. She looks back at the building once and then we lost her for good. So, either the Reaper knows where all the cameras are and is excellent at avoiding them, or he just blends into the crowd because we never see anyone that appears to be following her specifically. Though it's clear that she did speak to someone and whoever that was, she was obviously spooked," Melinda said.

"Well, at least we know that she left the station alive, though I don't know how long she'll stay that way if that was the Reaper she was talking to. I doubt he's going to settle for a friendly or not so friendly chat," Devon replied.

The three of them rifled through countless witness statements and took turns looking through traffic cams in the area in the hopes that anything would stand out, but after several hours, they still had little to go on.

Melinda and Piper decided to head home for the night, while Devon decided to order something for dinner and check on Mase and Dakota. When he discovered that everything was quiet upon reaching the hallway outside Mason's bedroom, he headed back downstairs to check with the officers outside and ordered a couple of pizzas, deciding to let them be until there was a reason to disturb them.

Kristi Loucks

Chapter 13

Mason pulled the covers up over Dakota before walking over towards the window to look out on the city streets. Normally, the bustling city brought him comfort, but at the moment, all he could think about was taking Dakota as far away as possible.

Realistically, he knew that there was no distance that would keep her safe. The only thing he could do was to find a way to catch the Reaper and do everything in his power to keep her and the rest of the people they cared about safe until then.

"You can't carry everyone's burden on your shoulders, Mase," Dakota whispered.

"I thought you were asleep," he said as he walked back to sit on the bed beside her.

"I was, but the sound of your brain whirring away is pretty hard to ignore."

"That bad?"

"I'm sorry for having a melt down on you. You were gone so long, and I didn't hear anything. All of the 'what ifs' started to take over in my head."

"Shh, don't apologize to me. Given the circumstances, I'd say a meltdown was inevitable. I'm just glad that I was there," he whispered as he leaned back against the pillows and wrapped his arms around her.

"I spent so much time trying to find my independence, and I succeeded, but today I realized that I want to depend on you and suddenly it dawned on me that someone else holds the cards in both of our fates. What if he finds you first? Or worse, what if this is someone that I know? What if he could walk right up to me and I have no idea that he's the person who could take you away from me?" she whispered. "I've been blind for a really long time, but there was never a time when I felt as if I couldn't 'see' until now. For all I know, he could sit in my diner and talk to me and the more I learn about the case, the more certain I am that I 'know' this man."

"Dakota, I promise you that we're going to find him. If I can't be with you myself, then I'll make sure that you are well covered. He won't get you alone."

"What if he gets you alone?" she asked quietly.

"He won't," Mason answered, trying to make it sound convincing, but he knew her concerns were all valid. "Right now, you're here with me. We have a state-of-the-art security system and a handful of cops within earshot. So, let's not think about what could happen for a little while, okay?"

"Okay," Dakota answered with a sigh as she settled closer to his side.

She was silent for a few minutes before she whispered, "When this is all over, can we go away somewhere?"

"Anywhere," he whispered, brushing his lips against her ear as he spoke.

"Someplace warm," she whispered as she finally fell back to sleep.

Mason listened to her even breathing as he thought about all of the places he'd love to take her, and before long, he was dreaming about the sun, sand, and Dakota.

About two hours later, Mason jumped as he heard a light tap on the door.

"It's open," he answered.

"Mase, I ordered some pizzas since no one has eaten dinner. I got a couple extras for the guys outside. You two should eat something and I'll fill you in on what Mel and Piper found."

"Did they leave?" Mason asked.

"Yeah, it's been a long day. They headed home for the night."

Mason woke Dakota and the three of them made their way into the kitchen to grab a bite to eat and discuss what had occurred in the last few hours.

"Any word on this Peter guy that the Beauford's met with?" Mason asked.

"Melinda is tracking him down. She thinks she's got a solid lead."

"Good. What else?"

"Okay, so we have no surveillance on Angela with this guy. It's possible he's on the surveillance footage, but since we have no idea what he looks like, that's a bust. We were hoping we'd get lucky enough to see him with Angela, at least, but he could be anyone really," Devon shared.

"What if we looked at surveillance from the last few weeks? I mean it's a train station. I'd be willing to bet at least ninety percent of the people on the footage are there Monday through Friday at the same times, since most of them are commuters. What if we looked for someone who isn't there regularly? It would at least narrow the field of suspects down to a more reasonable number," Mason offered.

"That's a good idea. I'll have the surveillance from the last month sent to the lab and have them do a more thorough analysis," Devon said.

"I think maybe it's time for you to meet my aunt and uncle," Dakota offered quietly.

"Do you think they might know something?" Mason asked.

"I don't know. It's possible. I can't believe I'm actually considering introducing you to this man, but the more I think about it the more certain I am that this might be someone I've crossed paths with, or knew, even. It seems likely that would have occurred when I lived with them. Besides, you don't blow up someone's house because of some deep-seated hatred of the man you're dating. Mase, I'd think he'd come after you more directly if that had been the case, or at least wait until I was in the house if he'd planned to use me to hurt you." Dakota gasped as the last thought left her mouth.

She had yet to voice that concern, but now it was out in the open and she had to deal with that truth. "What he did just put me closer to you and Devon, and ensured that his opportunities to get to me will be much harder to come by. I don't think that message was for you. I think it was for me. I think it was meant to scare me. Scaring you was just icing on the cake."

"Maybe he meant to scare both of you," Devon said. "I mean, think about it this way; what better way to gauge the seriousness of your relationship than to take a shot at both of you? See how you react. I'm guessing he knows where the two of you stand now. If he's after one of you, then he's likely after both of you. The question is, how did Mase get on his radar? We already know that you most likely had some contact with him as a kid," he finished as he touched Dakota's hand.

"Well, I think we need to see if we can figure out where that connection was made, and when. Then, see if we can't figure out if I knew him, and how well I might have known him," Dakota answered. "The only way to do that is to visit my aunt and uncle. And the only way I'm going there is if you two are coming with."

"Wouldn't have it any other way, love. Besides, I'm very much looking forward to having a chat with your uncle," Mason said as he looked to his brother, who appeared equally anxious to "introduce" himself to the man who had tormented Dakota.

"Well, we can't do anything until morning. If you don't mind, I'm just going to stay in the guest room. Then we can get a head start in the morning," Devon stated.

"Okay, do you want to call Piper and Melinda or should I?" Mason asked.

"I'll send them a text. They might already be sleeping," Devon answered as he pulled out his phone, texting as he headed up the stairs to the guest room.

Mason cleared up the plates from their dinner and loaded the dishwasher before leading Dakota back up to his bedroom.

Chapter 14

Melinda was exhausted when she arrived home. Despite the fact that there had been little progress on the case, there sure seemed to be an awful lot of work to do.

She climbed the stairs and unlocked her front door, but she immediately felt a draft waft out into the hallway as her door opened. A shiver ran down her spine, but she wrote it off as a normal reaction. It was hard not to be a little paranoid when you worked in law enforcement.

She reached over and turned on the lights to her right, then she turned back, locked both deadbolts, and dropped her bag on the floor. She shivered again and decided that she needed a hot shower to warm up. On her way back towards the bedroom, she remembered the window she'd cracked that morning when she burned her toast and laughed to herself over the uneasy feeling she'd allowed to take over. She shut the window and shook her head as she moved back towards the bedroom once again.

She turned on the water to let it warm up, headed back into the living room to check her voicemail, and grabbed her phone to charge it. That's when she noticed a text from Devon.

We're going to meet Dakota's aunt and uncle tomorrow; we'll swing by your place at 8 to pick you up. Piper is going to keep working on video footage and trying to track down the caseworker, Peter Donahue.

Melinda replied before setting the phone on the charger.

I made several calls today, so hopefully we'll have more by tomorrow. I think I may have found someone who knows Mr. Donahue.

She quickly pressed play on her answering machine. The first three messages were from her dry cleaners, the local pharmacy, and some guy her friend was trying to set her up with. The fourth message was an unfamiliar voice.

"Hello. This message is for a Melinda Kade. A friend of mine from Children's Services gave me your name and number. I understand that you are looking for more information on some of the cases that I handled during my time with CPS. I am not sure how much I can help you, as much of what we did is sealed to protect the children, but I would be happy to meet with you whenever you are available. Oh, I suppose it would help if I gave you my name. It's Peter Donahue. You can reach me at 312-555-1028."

Melinda looked at the clock and saw that it was a little before nine, so she called the number back.

"Hello."

"Hi. Is this Peter Donahue?"

"Yes it is. How can I help you?"

"This is Melinda Kade from the Serial Crimes Unit. I've been trying to get in touch with you."

"Oh, yes. What can I do for you?"

"I wanted to talk to you about some of the children that you worked with. It would be better if we could do it in person, and perhaps someplace where we could speak candidly," she offered.

"Ah, well, I don't get out much anymore. I was in an accident a number of years ago and I am now confined to a wheelchair, but you are more than welcome to visit me at home. I'd be happy to answer whatever questions I can."

"When can we meet? It is rather urgent," she said.

"Well, I suppose you could come out to the house now," the man said, and then gave her his address and directions to his home.

"Okay, I'll be there in twenty minutes," Melinda told the man.

"I'll look forward to your arrival," he answered before the call disconnected.

Melinda ran back and turned off the water before grabbing her cell phone and purse. She quickly made her way back out to her car and headed to meet Mr. Donahue.

When Melinda arrived, the house was dark apart from a single light at the door and one interior light towards the back of the house. She knocked lightly, hoping that Mr. Donahue hadn't fallen asleep given the late hour.

She was quickly reassured when a series of lights popped on as the man made his way to the front door. He clumsily maneuvered the chair around so that he could open the door for his guest.

"You must be Officer Kade. So nice to meet you in person," Mr. Donahue said.

"You, too. I'm glad we were able to locate you," she answered with a smile.

"Well, do come in. I just put on a pot of coffee. Can I interest you in a cup?"

"Sure, that sounds great."

"Come on back to the kitchen."

Melinda followed him back and watched as he set the pot on the table and motioned for her to take a seat.

He poured two cups of coffee and handed one to her before alerting her to the carafe of cream and sugar packets on the table.

Melinda poured a splash of cream into her coffee and let it sit for a few minutes to cool off.

She watched as Mr. Donahue added a healthy dose of cream to his coffee and took a big swallow of the warm liquid. A moment later, he asked, "So what is it that I can help you with?"

"Well, I was hoping you might have some information on some of the foster children that you were the primary caseworker for."

"Ah, well I can't talk about sealed cases."

"I understand that, but they are part of a murder case. Unfortunately, they are deceased, and we think that the man responsible may have also been one of your cases," she offered.

Melinda took a sip of her coffee as she waited for him to consider the information she'd given him.

"You say they are all deceased?" he asked.

"Well, no. But, I do believe that a number of them may be targets. Please, Mr. Donahue, I just need to see if they are interconnected and see if we can't perhaps pinpoint a suspect."

"I'll do my best," he answered as he cleared his throat and thumped his chest.

Melinda noticed tiny beads of sweat covered his brow. "Mr. Donahue, are you feeling all right?"

Clearing his throat again, he answered, "Yes. Yes, of course. I must be coming down with a cold or something. We should probably move our conversation into my office. That's where I keep my files."

"Oh, of course. I'll follow you."

Melinda carried both of their coffee cups into the office that was off the living room at the front of the house. She glanced out the front window on the way by and saw the unmarked car that had been assigned to her parked out front.

She set the coffee cups on the desk and took a seat as Mr. Donahue rummaged through the file cabinet beside his desk.

"Ah, here we go," he said, pulling a thick file from the drawer before gulping down the last of his coffee.

Melinda finished hers as well before she leaned over the desk to look at the file with Mr. Donahue. Before she started to ask questions, she opened a voice recording on her phone and held it in her lap as they spoke.

"Mr. Donahue, can you think of any children that might have been capable of violence?"

"Miss Kade, most of the children who enter the system have been exposed to violence at a young age. They all cope in different ways. Some retreat into themselves, some seem to be impervious to the abuse and some find ways to take it out on others. There were a number of children that were prone to violent outbursts, but I'm an old man. I don't remember everything about my cases as well as I used to. I'm sorry," he answered.

"Well, hopefully the files will tell us a little more," she answered with a reassuring smile.

"I hope so. You know I was responsible for these kids. I hate to think any of them capable of the kind of violence you see." He wheezed.

"Mr. Donahue, are you sure you're feeling all right?" she asked, noticing his pale coloration.

"Yes, dear, I'm fine. It's just this damn winter air and old age, I'm afraid," he answered.

Mr. Donahue had kept excellent records and followed each child from the time they had been removed from their home until they were permanently placed with a new family. He even had notes regarding their progress with their permanent families years later. Within fifteen minutes, they had come across the file of Jon Morrow, the young man she knew as Jonathon Beauford. There were a number of names that were linked to the boy, who had entered the system a year after his mother, Lauren Morrow, had passed away. He'd been placed with her sister, Darcy Harlow, but with a number of her own children, they decided it was more than they could handle.

After less than a year, he was placed with Gerald and Abigail Hagen for a brief time before the Beaufords officially adopted him. The Hagens had a niece in their care, Dakota Shelton, which confirmed what they already knew about Jon Beauford's connection to Dakota.

"You know, Jon Morrow had two cousins that ended up in foster care a few years later. Jason and Joseph...I believe those were their names."

Melinda stood to look through the stack of papers for more on the cousins when a wave of dizziness hit her hard.

"Perhaps, I can help you, Melinda," a voice stated from the doorway.

Melinda stood and spun towards the voice, but the movement completely destroyed what was left of her equilibrium, toppling her to the left as she fell to the floor.

She looked over at Mr. Donahue, who was unconscious and slumped over the stack of papers at his desk.

"Who...Who are you?" she stuttered.

"I am the answer to all of your questions," the man said with a wicked laugh. "I knew you'd eventually lead me to the elusive Mr. Donahue. Looks like a quick dose of diazepam did the trick nicely."

"You're the Reaper," she whispered.

She could hear a phone ringing and a garbled conversation as consciousness started to slip away.

"This is Mr. Donahue ..... nine o'clock .... California Avenue...." the Reaper spoke as the clouds of unconsciousness settled over Melinda. Her last thoughts were concern for the person on the other end of the line.

When Piper got home, he spoke with Mr. Donahue's former aide at Children's Services, who gave him a name and address for his mentor. Upon speaking to Mr. Donahue over the phone, he arranged to meet him the following morning around nine. He immediately sent a text to Devon, letting him know about his meeting and that he would check in with them, once he'd had a chance to speak to Mr. Donahue.

Neither one of them was aware of Melinda's meeting as she had been in too much of a hurry to alert them.

Chapter 15

As the haze of unconscious thought began to part, Melinda started to become aware of a presence in the room.

"I am so glad to see you coming around. I was afraid I was going to have to kill you without giving you a chance to enjoy the show," the Reaper said.

Melinda gasped as she realized the nightmare she'd been having was an awful lot better than her current reality as she tried to rub her forehead, only to find her hands had been bound tightly to a metal handrail in what appeared to be a bathroom, though she couldn't be certain with her muddled thoughts and the relative darkness.

"Where are we?" she whispered hoarsely as she tried and failed to take in her surroundings. Her vision was blurred by the bright lights and whatever he'd dosed her with.

"Oh, that is of no concern. Rest assured your partner . . . Torello, is it? He'll be here in the morning."

"No," she whispered as she thought about what might happen to her partner if he walked into this trap. "This can end with me."

"How very kind of you, but I have no intention of harming him. You see, I'll be long gone by the time he arrives. Unfortunately, so will any information that old coot had on me. And I don't intend to leave you in any state to tell him anything," he said as he dragged something across her cheek.

Melinda felt the warmth drip in a curtain down the side of her face and she knew exactly what he'd done, but confusion still hung around her, as she hadn't felt the blade open the wound she knew he'd inflicted.

"Pharmaceuticals really are the magic of the modern day, don't you agree?" the Reaper asked as he smiled ominously at Melinda.

Melinda's heart rate kicked up at that thought. In the darkness, she couldn't assess her current state. The harder she struggled, the more the feeling of numbness settled over her.

"What have you done to me?" she whimpered, her voice barely audible through the fog, as her head began to throb.

"I extended a kindness. You see, I can't have you screaming, and as much as I would enjoy it, I simply don't have time for a fight. I am on a tight schedule, after all. So, I gave you a little something to depress the central nervous system and of course, the diazepam can interrupt the pain receptors shooting towards your brain."

With that, he ran the blade across the other cheek, opening another gaping wound. The movement was fluid and well practiced.

Melinda fought with everything she had to stay conscious, praying that he would give her some opportunity at least to leave a clue.

For what seemed like hours, the Reaper spoke about his past and what had etched the darkness onto his soul. He provided her with all the information they would need to capture him, and she knew without a doubt that he would never allow her to survive long enough to divulge what she'd learned. With each clue came another shallow cut beneath her collarbones, across her sternum, over her shoulders, and across the tops of her forearms. None deep enough to kill on its own, but collectively, they were far more serious.

She could feel the rapidly cooling blood that soaked her clothing and pooled beneath her, and she knew that she was slowly bleeding out.

"You're a doctor. How can you do this?" she whispered on a gasp of air.

"It's quite easy, actually. I found that a man with my predilections could easily conceal his true nature behind the guise of a medical practitioner. Even though I don't practice medicine in the traditional sense." He laughed. "I have access to pharmaceuticals and tools, and even better, I can keep tabs on the investigations without creating suspicion."

Just then, Melinda heard a loud crash downstairs. Hope bloomed as she wondered who or what had made the sound.

The door opened and light poured in. Tears dripped from her cheeks as she assessed the situation. With all of the blood that covered her skin, it was hard to tell just how bad the injuries were, but she didn't appear to be losing blood quickly enough to indicate a major blood supply had been opened.

She heard another loud noise coming from downstairs, followed by Mr. Donahue's voice as he spoke the Reaper's name.

"Oh, you remember me. I'm touched, really. Consider this an act of mercy, old man," the Reaper said before Melinda heard a blood-curdling scream, followed by rapidly ascending footsteps as he made his return.

When the Reaper appeared in the doorway covered in blood, she knew the old man was dead.

"You'll never get out of here without being noticed. I have an unmarked car following me."

"Ah, yes. Well, I took the liberty of introducing myself to your tail earlier." He smiled. "They won't be a problem. Although, I should get back to them before your friend arrives. Speaking of which, I think I'd best be on my way."

Melinda was shocked when she felt her restraints drop free of the rail. She quickly pushed away from the wall in an effort to stand and advance on the Reaper.

He smiled down at her and laughed as he raised his right hand.

"Unfortunately, I just don't have the time to play. You understand, don't you?" he asked apologetically.

She saw the glint of the blade covered in blood that undoubtedly came from Peter Donahue just before it came down. Air rushed from her lungs as it pierced her skin. The sounds of metal and bone colliding and the feeling of said bones giving way to the blade like they were toothpicks was a surreal experience. She crumpled to the floor as her legs gave out and she gasped for what little air she could take into her burning lungs.

Before turning to leave, he yanked the curtain back on the window above her, revealing the early stages of the sunrise.

"You have about two hours until Torello arrives. If you last that long, then you deserve to live." He laughed sardonically as he jerked the blade from her chest and walked out of the room.

133

For the first time since she came to, the pain clung to her like a wet blanket in the dead of winter. She tried desperately to pull air into her lungs as she choked and gagged on the bitter metallic taste that now coated her tongue. Her hands immediately covered the wound as she attempted to slow the flow of blood. She fought for as long as she could to stay awake before she laid her head down and let the darkness consume her.

It was a little before eight when Piper's phone rang.

"Hello."

"Hey, Piper, it's Mase. Is Melinda with you?"

"No. I thought she was going with you today."

"So did I."

"Well, maybe she overslept?"

"Trust me, the way Dev's been banging on her door, she'd be up by now."

"She probably had a date, then. I'll tell you what; I'm meeting Peter Donahue at nine, then I'll find my wayward partner so she can do the walk of shame when you all get back." Piper laughed.

"Yeah, you're probably right, but I'm going to call down to the precinct and find out who was on her detail last night anyway."

"Okay, Mase. Call me if you find anything out," Piper said as he poured himself a glass of OJ.

"Will do."

Mason disconnected the call and looked at Devon and Dakota, who were still standing in the lobby of Melinda's building.

"What did he say?" Dakota asked.

"That she was probably going to have to do a walk of shame," Mason said. "Dev, can you call the precinct and see who was on her detail last night? They would have switched shifts at seven, so maybe they can tell us something."

Mason wrapped his arm around Dakota as he tried to dispel the uneasy feeling in the pit of his stomach and dialed Melinda's cell again. Still, there was no answer.

He listened to Devon as he spoke to the dispatcher. It was clear he wasn't getting an answer that he liked, based on the line that creased his forehead and the way he was pinching his nose. When he finished the call, he turned towards Mason and said, "We've got a problem."

"Dev, take Dakota to my place and stay there until you hear from me," Mason ordered as he dialed Piper.

He kissed her forehead before helping her into Dev's car and whispered, "I'll be back as soon as I can."

As soon as her door was closed, Mason hit send and watched as Devon drove off.

"Where was she?" Piper laughed as soon as he picked up.

"Her team never checked in for the shift change," Mason said.

"What! How long ago were they supposed to check in?"

"Between six and seven this morning. Piper, I need you to pick me up at Melinda's. Dispatch had them checking in here, so she made it home. The super at Melinda's building just got here. So, I'm going to take a look around her apartment and see if I can't figure out where she was headed from here. The dispatcher is going to pull the GPS records for the unit that was with her last night, so hopefully by the time you get here, we'll know where to look," Mason said before he hung up to greet the super.

Mason held up his badge as the super approached and unlocked her door.

"Thank you. I'll lock up when I leave," Mason told the man in a not-so-subtle dismissal.

Mason walked over to her answering machine and pressed play, listening to a few pointless messages while he walked around her apartment. As he headed back into the kitchen, he heard the last message and stopped in his tracks. It was from Peter Donahue, the caseworker that had placed Jonathon Beauford. The same man Piper had planned to meet that morning.

He was sprinting down the steps while talking to a clerk at the precinct, trying to get an address for Mr. Donahue.

"D-o-n-a-h-u-e, first name Peter. I need an address, YESTERDAY!" he barked as he ran straight into Piper.

"Mase, I already have his address. Is that where she went last night?" Piper asked.

"Never mind, we have the address. Just tell dispatch to find the team that was with her ASAP!" Mason said before hanging up on her.

"They still haven't heard from them? What about the GPS on the unit?"

"Disabled."

Piper looked at him, knowing that wasn't a good sign.

As soon as they got on the road, Mason flipped the lights and sirens; he then picked up the radio and called in the address for back up and an ambulance.

They sped across town to Peter Donahue's address and parked in the first spot they could find. Mason was halfway up the block before Piper had even exited the vehicle.

When he got to Donahue's house, he pulled out his gun and carefully made his way up the front steps. As soon as he heard Piper creep up the steps behind him, he turned the handle and pushed on the door. It was unlocked, which was another bad sign.

Once they'd entered the foyer of the home, they knew something was horribly wrong. The house was virtually silent and the pungent odor of blood hung in the air. Mason took lead as he edged his way from room to room until he came upon a man he suspected was Peter Donahue. He bent down and checked for a pulse, shaking his head when he glanced back at Piper. The man was dead; his throat had been slashed from ear to ear after his eyes had been gouged out.

Clearly, this wasn't his usual MO. They were quickly learning that the Reaper made a habit out of getting exceedingly violent with the people he held personally responsible for his suffering. It seemed he was much more refined in his methods when he was killing the people he felt had avoided the path he'd been forced to travel on.

After they secured the rest of the main floor, Mason started to work his way up the stairs with Piper backing him up. He noticed the stair lift and remembered a broken wheelchair they had seen in the office where they'd found beside Donahue.

They started with the rooms at the front of the house and worked their way to the rooms at the back of the house, checking for any sign of an assailant still lurking in the home. When they got to the last two doors, Piper took one and Mason took the other.

Piper breathed a sigh of relief as he checked the bedroom and both closets, and he made his way back towards the hallway.

As soon as the bathroom door popped open, Mason dropped to his knees next to Melinda, who was lying on her side. Her clothes were saturated and the blood on the floor was dark and sticky. She'd been here for some time.

He carefully placed his fingers on her neck to feel for a pulse just as he heard Piper come around the corner. Seconds later, her eyes fluttered open. They both saw what appeared to be a large penetrating stab wound just below the sternum.

Mason grabbed a towel from the counter and used it to apply pressure to the wound.

"I need an ETA on that ambulance and where the fuck was her team!!" Mason shouted to Piper.

He heard Piper yelling into his phone before he turned back to Melinda.

"I'm going to go downstairs to flag them down!" Piper said as he ran down the stairs.

Mason lifted her from the floor and cradled her in his arms, using the leverage to keep pressure on her wound.

He whispered, "I've got you. You're going to be okay. Just hang on for me."

Tears dripped from her eyes as she looked at him and he tried as hard as he could not to let her see the crippling fear that was clawing at his chest in that moment.

"An ambulance is on the way, Mel. They'll be here any minute," he said as he felt the sting of tears in his own eyes.

Melinda was barely gasping for air as blood crowded her airway when she tried to say something.

"Shh. Don't try to talk. Just stay with me," Mason said to her.

She tried to pull herself up closer to him, and he knew that her struggling was doing more harm, so he carefully lifted her up close enough that he could hear her.

She tried to speak once again, but as she exhaled, blood clogged her throat, making it impossible to speak. She grabbed hold of Mason's hand and frantically traced the letters MD over and over.

"MD? Initials?"

She didn't get a chance to answer as exhaustion began to take over and her lungs filled with blood.

"You're going to be okay," he whispered.

"I can hear the ambulance," he lied as his shoulders began to shake.

"S'ok...ay. Mase..." she choked out as she gasped for a breath that simply wouldn't make it to her lungs.

"No. No. No! You stay with me. Don't you say goodbye," Mason whispered.

He watched her as she closed her eyes and a few moments later, she took one more gasping breath before everything just stopped. Mason carefully laid her on the floor and started chest compressions; panic was building as his heart pumped furiously with a surge of adrenaline.

As the sounds of the ambulance got closer, he finally let go of the scream that had been trapped in his lungs since he'd found her on that bathroom floor.

"Mason!! Mase?" He heard Piper call as he sprinted up the steps.

When he finally came to a stop in the doorway, he saw Mason frantically trying to keep her alive.

"Where's the ambulance?" Mason barked as he continued CPR.

Piper just stood there in shock for a moment before he disappeared at the sound of banging on the door.

The EMTs entered the room moments later, dropping heavy bags and starting to assess the injuries. The first one checked her pulse and flashed a penlight to check her pupils. He immediately pulled adhesive paddles, an ambubag, and an IV from his bag before cutting away the sweater and attaching the paddles.

The medic looked up at his partner and yelled, "Check him!"

"I'm fine. It's her blood," Mason said as he pushed back and leaned against the far wall.

He watched as the pair of medics established an IV line and intubated Melinda. Her chest began to rise and fall as one of them depressed the bag.

"Sir, I need your help. I want you to squeeze the bag on counts of three, like this: 1-2-3, breathe. 1-2-3, breathe. Got it?" he asked.

"Got it," Mason said as he watched the medic leave the room and return with a backboard.

"Okay, on three, we're going to roll her toward us so that Jim can get the backboard under her," the other medic said firmly.

"One, two, three!" he bellowed. Once the board was in place, he resumed his count with the bag while one of the medics tightened the straps. Within a few minutes, they were loading Melinda into the ambulance.

"Sir, I need you to ride with us. Your friend can follow," Jim said to Mason.

"We're headed to Northwestern," the medic yelled to Piper.

Mason nodded and climbed in next to Melinda and continued with the ambubag.

Jim climbed in, slamming the doors before turning to watch the monitor carefully as he relayed information to the hospital.

"Female, mid-twenties. Pulse is weak and thready....."

Mason tuned out the sound of the medic talking as he focused on Melinda. "Hang on for me, Mel. We're almost there," he whispered.

They managed to travel a few miles before the monitors started to wail and the ambulance came to a stop. They spent almost ten minutes working tirelessly to keep blood pumping before they finally got a pulse.

The rest of the ride was excruciating, and he never let his gaze stray from the monitors to Melinda's right. Thankfully, they made it without another incident, but Mason knew she was far from out of the woods.

When they arrived at the hospital, the medic opened the doors and carefully released the gurney from the track, pulling it from the vehicle. Instantly, doctors and nurses who were rapidly firing off questions surrounded them.

Mason followed as he glanced around for Piper. When he didn't see him, he just continued to follow the medics as they moved Melinda to a curtained room.

He sat in a chair just outside the curtained off area where they'd taken Melinda and watched as the doctors and nurses hastily scurried about ordering labs and prepping his friend for the inevitable surgery to try to fix the damage the Reaper had done.

"Sir. Sir?" a nurse said as she entered the room. "Would you like to get cleaned up?"

He glanced down at his hands, quickly realizing that he was covered in Melinda's blood. He looked up at the nurse and nodded before he stood to follow her into another room that looked like a locker room. She handed him a pair of clean scrubs just as he heard Devon come into the room, sounding absolutely frantic.

"Where's my brother?" he all but screamed.

"Oh, thank God," he said as he saw his brother standing in the adjacent bathroom.

When he rounded the corner, his elation turned to horror as he saw all of the blood that clung to his clothes and his skin.

"Are you okay? Piper? Melinda?" he asked.

"I'm fine. I thought Piper called you. How did you know if you haven't talked to him?" Mason wondered.

"Dr. Hovey called me. She had only heard that there was a body and a survivor at Donahue's home. She's on her way there now."

Devon stared at his brother, waiting for an answer, but it didn't come. He just looked so...broken.

In an instant, Devon was looking frantic. "What is it, Mase? What's going on? Are you hurt?" he asked as he began to catalog the blood that stained Mason's clothing and skin once again.

Mason shook his head as tears welled in his eyes. "It's Melinda."

"How bad?" Devon asked as his voice cracked and his throat started to burn.

"It's bad, Dev. Really bad. Center mass penetrating stab wound."

"Was she conscious?"

"She was when I got to her. But she coded twice. The last time, we almost didn't get her back."

"I need to see her," Devon said as he turned for the door.

"You don't want to do that, Dev. You really don't."

"I have to."

Mason nodded and led his brother back towards the curtained off area.

The doctors had just pulled it back and were pushing the gurney out into the hallway as they started to head towards the OR.

Mason moved to the side and watched as his brother moved towards Melinda.

"Oh God," Devon whispered as he took in the sickly pallor of her skin.

Her eyes were winged by severe shadows that told of the horrors of her last several hours; the horrors that occurred while the rest of the world slept peacefully.

A few minutes later, a nurse came by and led them to a private waiting area where Piper sat talking to another police officer, undoubtedly recalling the circumstances that had led them all here.

Mason looked back at his brother with panic as he realized a key point. "Where's Dakota? I thought you were going to stay with her!"

"I took her to the diner. We sent an extra unit over with her. I couldn't sit back and wait without knowing everyone was...." He stopped short because everyone was most definitely not okay.

"What does she know? She's got to be in a panic."

"I told her that you needed back up. I didn't tell her there was a body," Devon said, feeling a little guilty for his lie of omission.

Mason glared at his brother for a moment and said, "Go talk to the cop. I'll be back after I get cleaned up."

Chapter 16

He headed back to the lounge and stepped out of his bloody clothes. When he got down to his boxers, a door opened and a nurse stood there, looking stunned. "I'm sorry. I didn't. I mean. The officer said to tell you that your clothes need to be admitted into evidence."

She walked over to where he stood, trying not to stare at him and handed him a plastic bag before she scurried off again while apologizing again.

Mason dumped the clothes into the bag and set it aside before stepping into the nearby shower stall and rinsing the blood from his skin. No matter how hot the water was or how much he scrubbed, the coppery tang of blood still lingered in the steam around him. He didn't know how long he'd been in there, but after a while, he slid down the cool tile to the floor as reality violently took hold.

"Mase, you okay?" Dev called from the doorway.

When Devon didn't get an answer, he sprinted towards the sounds of running water. A rush of cold air assaulted Mason as he looked up at his brother's worried face. "Mase, you scared the crap out of me. When I left Dakota, she told me to bring you home or face a penalty of death. So, I'm bringing you home if it kills me."

Mason cracked a little smile at the comment.

"What? She scares me a lot more than you do. She's like a ninja. She can probably find me using one of her other superhuman senses," he said as he threw a towel at Mase and helped him stand.

Mason laughed aloud and Devon turned back, "On second thought, I don't want to know what kind of heightened senses she has." Devon walked back out of the room. He smiled to himself a little as he left. "My work here is done," he said to the nurse who had asked him to check on his brother.

Mason threw on the scrubs and headed back to the waiting area where Piper and Devon were talking to two uniformed officers. He handed them the bag with his clothing and sat down beside his brother.

"Do we know anything yet?"

"No. She's still in surgery. Probably will be for several more hours," Devon stated.

"What about you guys? Anything?" he asked the two officers.

"Dr. Hovey transported the male vic back to autopsy. Looks like they were drugged. There was residue in the two coffee cups that were in the office. I'm sure the lab will have more for you shortly. Robin sent us down to grab your clothes and Melinda's with instructions to bring them to the lab immediately. And we wanted to take statements while it was still fresh in everyone's mind," one of the officers said.

"And her protective detail? Where were they when all of this went down?" Mason asked.

"Dead. Found a few miles from the house with their throats slit," the second officer said.

"Son of a bitch," Mason swore as he sent the magazines flying from the table.

Thirty minutes later, Mason had given his account of what happened to the officers who stood and made their way back to the lab as instructed, leaving the three of them in the waiting room.

Mason let his mind wander over the events of the day when he had a thought. He reached for his cell phone and realized it was still in his pants pocket.

"Here, use mine." Devon said as he handed it over, assuming he was going to call Dakota.

"Robin, good I'm glad I caught you," Mason practically shouted.

Devon and Piper just stared as they tried to figure out what Mason was after.

"What's going on? I haven't even gotten the evidence yet. Is she okay?" the lab tech babbled.

Mason completely ignored all of it. "Check her phone!"

"What? I don't have it yet."

144

"When you get it, check for an audio file," Mason answered impatiently.

"Okay. What are you looking for?"

"Her audio notes from the conversation with Donahue. And if we're lucky, maybe the Reaper will have a cameo," Mason answered. "She's still in surgery, by the way. I'll make sure someone updates you as soon as we know more."

"Okay. We'll call you as soon as there is anything of note."

"Thank you," Mason answered before hanging up.

He handed the phone back to Devon, who studied his brother for a moment.

"You don't want to call Dakota?"

"Oh, I do. But, whatever I tell her is just going to have her even more worried. I'll call her when we have some news," he answered.

Devon nodded and put the phone away.

After another hour passed, Mason stood up and paced the hallway. He was torn between needing to be there in case there was an update and seeing Dakota. He knew that she was probably worried about all of them.

Devon finally walked up to him and said, "Come on. Let's go get Dakota because I can't stand watching you pace a hole in the floor anymore."

Mason looked between Devon and Piper, who quickly said, "I'll call if I hear anything. Go!"

Twenty minutes later, Devon's car was idling at the curb in front of the diner with the hazards on as the two of them went inside to get Dakota.

"Oh my God, we've been worried sick," Judy said when she spotted Mason.

Before Judy even finished her sentence, Mason had locked onto Dakota, sitting at their usual table, and headed in her direction.

She stood and turned towards the sound of his footsteps just as he lifted her into his arms and the fight drained out of him. She was instantly aware of the change in his demeanor as she felt his hot tears against her cheek.

"Mason, are you okay? What's wrong?" she whispered.

145

He sat in the booth, pulled her into his lap, and clung to her, shaking with exhaustion, fear, and anger.

"Want me to tell her?" Devon offered as he took a seat across from them.

Judy set some coffee on the table before she went to flip the "closed" sign and lock up. She refilled the officer's coffee at the counter and joined them, along with Molly.

"Melinda is in surgery. We're going to head back there soon..." Devon started.

"I didn't want to worry you, but I needed to see you. Will you come with us to the hospital?" Mason asked.

"Of course I will. You should have called me sooner," she whispered as she kissed his forehead.

"We'll come sit with you, too," Molly said. "I'll put together some coffee and stuff and Judy, Colleen, and I will come down."

"That would be nice," Devon said. "Mase, do you want to go home and get some clothes?"

"What's wrong with your clothes?" Dakota wondered as her hands slid down to his side.

"I had to change into a pair of scrubs. My clothes were evidence."

"Oh God, you were there?" Dakota asked. Her concern had quickly reappeared.

"Yes, but the Reaper was long gone by the time I got there," Mason assured them.

"I'll grab your coat, Dakota," Devon said as he headed back to the office.

They made their way to the house, where Mason jumped out and quickly changed into his own clothes, which went a long way towards making him feel better.

He rejoined Dakota and Devon in the car and they returned to the hospital.

When they entered the waiting room, Piper was sitting with Judy, Molly, and Colleen. They'd arrived with an arsenal of caffeine and pastries. Just what they needed since they'd been running on nothing for most of the day. It was already well past seven, almost twelve hours since he'd discovered something was terribly wrong.

"Any updates yet?" Mason asked.

146

Piper shook his head. "A nurse came by about forty minutes ago and told me that they were still working to repair the damage. She said Mel was lucky because it somehow missed her heart, but she has a punctured lung and a lot of internal bleeding. That was really all she told me."

"At least she's still fighting," Mason said.

"She's too stubborn to die," Piper added.

"Let's hope," Devon whispered, refilling his coffee.

Silence fell over the room, and the group went back to staring at the door as if to will a doctor to come through with news. It was another two hours before one actually did, and it wasn't the doctor they'd been hoping for.

"How is she?" Dr. Hovey asked as she walked in.

"We don't know. It's been hours since we've heard anything," Mason said.

"Well, hon. Take that as good news. There's still something to fight for if they aren't in here talking to us," she added.

Judy came over and handed her a cup of coffee and a scone before heading back to her seat.

"I see what the fuss is about. I guess it's good to have reinforcements that carry thermoses of coffee and baked goods," she said as she smiled at the older woman.

"You have no idea," Devon said as he helped himself to yet another cup of coffee.

The group talked as they tried hard not to think about what was taking so long. Finally, after another twenty minutes, a doctor came into the room.

The man glanced around the room until he saw Mason and said, "Well, Melinda is critical, but she's still fighting. We managed to repair the damage to her lung, but we did have to remove a portion of the posterior basal lobe of her right lung and her spleen in order to control the hemorrhaging. Aside from the major trauma, she also had a number of smaller wounds that became problematic due to the sheer volume of blood loss. The next twenty-four to forty-eight hours are going to be crucial."

"When can we see her?" Mason asked.

"She's still in recovery. We'll be moving her to the ICU in a few hours, so it won't be until morning and she will only be allowed one visitor at a time. You should all go home and get some sleep in the meantime."

"I'm going to need to post two officers outside her room at all times," Mason said.

"I will let hospital security know. In the meantime, if you have any questions, please feel free to have one of the nurses page me," the doctor said before he went back to check on Melinda.

Relief flooded the thoughts of everyone in the room as they talked with Dr. Hovey about the new information. She assured them that despite how awful the surgery sounded, she was coming away from it with the best possible outcome. It hadn't damaged her heart or any other vital organs that she couldn't function without, though they all knew that she was still a long way from being out of the woods.

So, the group gathered up their belongings and headed to their cars, leaving the leftover coffee and pastries for the ER staff on the way out.

Mason and Dakota rode with Devon back to Mason's place and Piper headed home with a police escort. After the morning's events, they stayed in the house with Piper rather than out front. No one wanted to take any more chances.

Mason walked up the stairs with Dakota on his arm and Devon on their heels. Their police detail was stationed inside the house as well, with two at the front door and two at the back.

Mason quietly walked into his room, shutting the door behind them before carefully lifting Dakota in his arms as he toed off his shoes near the door. He pulled the covers back and set her on the edge of the bed before he leaned down and stole her breath away with a heated kiss.

His hands felt the rapid beat of her pulse as he slid them under the curtain of her hair to rest against her neck. The air crackled with electricity between them as he deepened their kiss, pulling her closer. His thoughts had been consumed with so much darkness, but Dakota reminded him of all the things that were still right in his world.

Her hands were cool against his skin as they skimmed beneath his t-shirt, landing on his lower back, but it wasn't enough. Mason reached back towards his shoulder and pulled his shirt forward and over his head before he helped Dakota to unbutton her shirt. His fingers softly pushed the material back past her collarbones and down her arms until it fluttered to the floor next to his shirt.

A sigh escaped past her lips as his tongue traced the lines of her collarbone, settling in the tiny indent at the base of her throat, making her shiver with anticipation.

Dakota's fingers tangled in his hair as he fanned the flames a little more by kissing his way down her breastbone and back up again until his mouth covered hers.

She shuddered as she thought about how well this man read her. Every touch, every kiss hit the mark and made her burn for him.

"I love you so much," he whispered as kissed her just below her earlobe.

She was certain he could feel her pulse thundering beneath his lips as he lingered there. His hands deftly flicked open the clasp against her back before he lifted her once more and settled her in the center of his bed, tossing the silky scrap of fabric over his shoulder.

When she felt the mattress dip under his weight, she quickly reached out and pushed him back against the pillows, allowing her hands to map every inch of his exposed skin, from the perfect dimple in his right cheek to his soft lips and the angle of his jaw. She leaned forward and rubbed her soft skin over the roughness of his jaw before her lips made the same circuit he had treated her to moments earlier.

His pulse thundered under her touch as she followed the muscled ridges of his shoulder down to his perfectly sculpted chest. Her hands traced the lines of his abs as they quivered under her attention until she reached the cool metal of his belt buckle.

Her hands shook as she pulled the belt free and dropped it to the floor with a soft clang. When her fingers returned to the button of his jeans, he stopped her while he sat up and pulled his knees up behind her until she reclined against them.

Mason leaned towards her so he could gently ease her legs forward to extend out behind him on the bed before he went about removing her jeans and discarding them.

He leaned into her, his hands sliding underneath her shoulder blades as he brought her forward, allowing the heat of her skin to permeate the cold that had settled over him that morning. All the while, her heart was fluttering like a hummingbird against his chest.

Dakota let her hands paint a picture of the man before her, smoothing the lines that had been etched in his forehead and chasing the shadows that had settled beneath his eyes.

"I never gave much thought to the possibility of finding someone like you," she whispered. "But now that you're here with me, I can't remember what my life was like before you."

She kissed him softly before she said, "You can't leave me now, okay?"

"Baby, I couldn't leave you if my life depended on it. Maybe not even if yours did, I'm just not that strong," he whispered against her ear, turning her so that she rested back against the pillows.

Dakota listened intently as she tried to gauge his next move, when she heard his pants drop to the floor and felt his weight as he climbed back towards her once again.

She could hear the lamp shake gently as he pulled the drawer open and the sound of plastic beneath his fingers as his hand lay on the bed beside her to support his weight. Each tiny noise she heard only added to the anticipation that was already alive within her.

His breath fell rapidly against her skin as he lightly scraped his teeth against the column of her neck while his hands were at her hips, gently easing the last thin scrap of silk that separated them down her legs.

Before she'd even had time to register his movement, he was beneath her again, as she heard his teeth tear into the plastic. She shivered as she listened to the subtle sounds around her until his hands found their way to her hips, lifting her small frame and guiding her movements over him.

Without a word, Dakota followed the pressure of his fingertips as he pulled her down into a kiss that quickly had them both breathless. His left hand was flat against the tiny dimples that framed her spine, while his right hand ghosted

150

feather light touches over her shoulder and down her arm, placing her hand against his chest for leverage.

The room was heavy with tension as he rose up to a sitting position, bringing Dakota closer and allowing himself to slip further into her as he gently sunk his teeth into the space between her shoulder and her neck, making her shudder against him.

Mason could feel the coil as it stretched taut, just waiting to snap free, but he wasn't ready yet.

He pulled back and eased her down once more; a question hung on her tongue until she felt his breath on her inner thigh. His tongue blazed a trail from her knee to her hipbone. Shifting his weight, Mason pressed his tongue firmly against her clit until her hips bucked up off the bed. The pressure was relentless as he slid two fingers into her, feeling her walls clamp down almost instantly as her fingernails abraded his shoulders.

"Mason," she wailed breathlessly while his other hand gently covered her mouth. Her whole body bowed from the mattress as she shook with pleasure.

Dakota felt the bed dip as Mason settled back between her thighs and picked up a more urgent rhythm as he laced his fingers with hers, kissing every inch of flesh within his reach. Heat flashed over him as he did everything he could to silence the groan that was threatening to burst free, but the second he felt the pressure of her heels pulling him forward and her teeth as they grazed his shoulder, all was forgotten.

"Oh fuck me," he gritted out as he felt her clamp down around him, tugging on that coil until it snapped violently. His whole body shook with every breath as they both rode out each little aftershock, sharing soft and lethargic kisses until he finally eased away.

She listened as she heard the water come on for a moment, then it shut off again. A few seconds later, Dakota felt the bed dip as Mason pulled her back into his arms and pulled the sheet back up around their hips.

"Did you miss me, love?" he crooned as he settled in behind her.

"Every second," she answered as she turned in his arms and laid a kiss over his heart. It still fluttered wildly, making her smile as she let her head rest against the pillow beside his.

Mason brushed her hair over her shoulder before he finally closed his eyes and let the exhaustion that had been threatening to take over all day consume him.

A calm finally settled over the house, but they all knew that when the sun came up, chaos would be waiting for them.

Chapter 17

A knock sounded on the door just after sunrise.

Mason stretched and pulled Dakota closer as he waited for Devon to knock again.

He did right before he cracked the door and stuck his head in, eyes closed, and said, "Come downstairs and get something to eat."

"We'll be down in a few," Mason said as he sat up.

"The good news is you slept through the shift change, so you don't have to do the walk of shame," Devon added as Mason threw a pillow that hit the door just after he'd closed it again.

"Stay here. I'll get you some clothes."

Dakota clutched the blankets to her chest as she curled up against the warmth he'd left behind. When he returned, he handed her a t-shirt and a pair of leggings. She quickly dressed and giggled when she stood and found the t-shirt grazed her knees, confirming it belonged to Mason.

"It looks way better on you, love," he whispered as he kissed her forehead and wrapped his hand gently around her elbow as he led her to the door.

Devon was sitting at the table facing the stairs when he saw his brother and Dakota come down. Piper was lurking near the coffee pot, but he smiled when he saw Devon practically vibrating with the need to trade barbs with his brother. He could tell something had gone down last night.

It was impossible for Devon not to make light of their evening activities; after all, it was a much brighter topic than the other elephant in the room.

"So, Mase," Devon said as he wound up for the pitch.

"Dev," Mason answered as he poured a cup of coffee for Dakota.

"Did you have a hard time getting to sleep last night?" Devon said.

Piper laughed as he thought of a cartoon where the villain twists his mustache. He could almost see Devon doing just that.

Mason started to respond, but Dakota beat him to it. "Actually, Dev, it wasn't the sleeping that was hard," she deadpanned as Piper choked on a mouthful of hot coffee.

"Shit, I love this girl," Piper said as he walked over and kissed her cheek.

"Yeah, okay. I walked right into that. You're killing my game, Dakota." Devon laughed.

Mason just smiled as he watched his brother try to formulate a new plan of attack.

An hour later, the four of them made their way up to the ICU to meet with Melinda's surgeon and see how she fared through the night.

"Good morning," the doctor said as he looked up from Melinda's chart at the nurse's station.

"Good morning," Mason said. "How is she doing?"

"Well, she's spiked a fever, so we're treating her with antibiotics to try and get ahead of it. It's not completely unexpected, but given the circumstances it's concerning," he said.

"Has she woken up at all?" Piper asked.

"No. She's still pretty heavily sedated. We'll start backing off the sedation tonight if she remains somewhat stable."

"Can I see her?" Mason asked.

"Of course. One at a time," the doctor responded as he led them to her room.

Mason walked in and sat in the chair beside Melinda. He reached up and held her hand as he took in her appearance. She was pale, and there were several large tubes that were draining fluid from her chest. Her hair was still matted with blood and her body was covered in bandages where the Reaper had cut into her flesh.

Mason leaned his forehead against the rail as he spoke, "I'm so sorry, Mel. I'm so sorry that I wasn't there earlier. You should have called me. Someone should have been with you. Why didn't you call one of us?" he wondered aloud.

After a few minutes, he stepped out and let the rest of the team sit with her for a bit.

Dakota sat with her last as Mason stood outside of the door.

"You know, there have only been a handful of times that I was truly thankful that I couldn't see, and two of them have occurred in the last couple of weeks. Right now, I know I am thinking of you happy and healthy because I know that the alternative probably isn't that great, especially when I felt the pain radiating off of Mason when he came to the diner last night. He loves you like he loves Devon, maybe more since you don't look for every opening to embarrass him." She smiled.

"I can hear you, Dakota," Devon said.

"Please, get better. Don't leave me to fend for myself with these men." She laughed as Mason, Devon, and Piper laughed, too.

She stood and walked into the hall, where she wrapped her arms around Mason.

The doctor came back and Dakota said, "Can I stay with her?"

"Sure. It might be good for her to hear someone she knows talking to her."

"Dakota, I'm not sure that's a good idea," Mason said.

"There are two officers here at all times, right? There is hospital security, too. I'm in no more danger than I would be at work," she argued. "You can't be with me all the time, but someone should be with her."

Everything in Mason told him to force her to leave, but he couldn't do it. He knew she was right. Someone needed to stay with Melinda.

"Okay, please call me if there's any change or if you need anything," he said as he kissed her forehead.

"I will, Mase. Just do what you need to do to catch this guy."

"Love you," he whispered.

"I love you, too."

With that, she made her way back to Melinda's bedside, holding her hand out until she reached the chair. She turned the television on to drown out the whooshing of the ventilator and the various pings from all of the machines, but her mind never strayed far from her friend beside her.

Mason rode in silence with Devon and Piper down to the lab. He was quickly greeted by an overly caffeinated version of Andy and Robin, who seemed thrilled to have some kind of a buffer.

"So what can you tell me?" Mason asked as he got straight down to business.

"Well, I checked her phone. There was an audio file. We cleaned it up as best we could," Robin offered as she led them to the conference room, where she cued it up.

"So this is a good news, bad news scenario. Which would you like first?" she said as she waited for the file to load.

"The recording includes the conversation with Mr. Donahue," Robin started.

"Hold on, that sounds like good news," Piper interrupted.

Robin glared at Piper and continued, "Unfortunately, Mr. Donahue didn't get to the important details. All we got is that Jon Morrow had two cousins who had landed in the system a year or so later."

"Still not sounding like bad news," Devon interjected.

"It's not all bad, I mean that's a hell of a lot more than we had yesterday, but without a little more info we don't know anything about the cousins," Robin replied.

"So, is that when the Reaper made his presence known?" Mason asked.

"Yes, he interrupted their conversation and here's the good news. Melinda somehow managed to keep her cell phone concealed and actually caught a fair amount of her conversation with the Reaper," Robin shared.

"So, what did he say?" Piper questioned impatiently.

"Quite a bit," Robin said.

She queued up the audio and played the recording back for the group.

The group listened intently as Peter Donahue and Melinda discussed Jon Morrow, whom they'd known as Jonathon Beauford. But, disappointment bloomed as the Reaper interrupted before the pair could delve further into the two cousins. Robin's initial assessment had been true; little had been said that they weren't already aware of with regards to Mr. Donahue.

Of course, they'd learned of the existence of the cousins, Jason and Joe, but there hadn't been time to garner more information as whatever drugs had been in play had effectively silenced the gentleman.

Once the Reaper's voice filled the room, the conversation took on a completely different tone. They listened as he addressed Melinda by her first name with a modicum of familiarity.

"Perhaps, I can help you, Melinda,"

"Who...Who are you?" she stuttered.

"I am the answer to all of your questions," the Reaper said. *"I knew you'd eventually lead me to the elusive Mr. Donahue. Looks like a quick dose of diazepam did the trick nicely."*

"You're the Reaper," she whispered.

As they listened carefully, a phone rang and it seemed the Reaper answered, pretending to be Mr. Donahue.

"This is Mr. Donahue," the Reaper said. *"Nine o'clock,"* he responded to the caller. *"California Avenue."*

Piper stopped the recording as he spoke up. "I talked to him. I was on the other end of that call!"

"You couldn't have known it was him," Devon said.

"Wait, what did you say?" Mason asked.

"I asked if I could speak to Donahue. I asked him what time was a good time to meet with him, and I also asked him what the nearest cross street was. Then I hung up. I should have known something was wrong when he was so abrupt with his answers," Piper responded as he pinched the bridge of his nose.

"Listen, there is no way you could have known that you were speaking to the Reaper, or that Mel was there," Mason told Piper before indicating for Robin to restart the audio.

The next thing they heard was the sound of a body being dragged away. It was clear that she hadn't been moved far from the room, as the recording continued to pick up the ambient noises, but clearly, he needed her out of the way. Mason wasn't positive it had been Melinda being dragged, but he assumed it was Melinda as it would have been easy to move a man in the wheelchair, though it was still unclear how the older man had ended up on the floor.

The Reaper moved swiftly around the office and began rustling through the papers and files, hastily scattering them about. The sounds were easily discernible, as was the sound of the Reaper becoming more frustrated by the second.

After several minutes of movement, a deep groan was heard, making it clear that Peter Donahue was starting to come around, but the sounds halted abruptly with a loud thump. Undoubtedly, the Reaper had sent the man back to his unconscious state.

With that, it sounded as though he had hefted Melinda up from the floor and headed up to the bathroom, where Mason had eventually found her. His labored breathing and the heavy thump of his boots were clear as he climbed the stairs, followed by the unmistakable whir of zip ties being secured to keep her immobilized while he took his time with her.

After a few minutes of silence, Melinda's breathing seemed to pick up as awareness started to filter back in.

"I am so glad to see you coming around. I was afraid I was going to have to kill you without giving you a chance to enjoy the show," the Reaper said.

"Where are we?" she whispered hoarsely.

"Oh, that is of no concern. Rest assured your partner . . . Torello, is it? He'll be here in the morning."

"No. This can end with me."

"How very kind of you, but I have no intention of harming him. You see, I'll be long gone by the time he arrives. Unfortunately, so will any information that old coot had on me. And I don't intend to leave you in any state to tell him anything," the Reaper said.

Mason heard a sharp intake of breath, and had to assume that the Reaper had made one of his first cuts. He clenched his fists as he tried to prepare himself for what was to come.

"Pharmaceuticals really are the magic of the modern day, don't you agree?"

"What have you done to me?" she whimpered.

They could hear her voice growing weaker with each breath, more defeated. Mason wondered if she had resigned herself to the promise of her death.

"I extended a kindness. You see, I can't have you screaming, and as much as I would enjoy it, I simply don't have time for a fight. I am on a

tight schedule, after all. So, I gave you a little something to depress the central nervous system and of course, the diazepam can interrupt the pain receptors shooting towards your brain."

They could hear the sounds of swift movements and small gasps as he clearly inflicted further injuries and it was hard not to cringe at the thought of just how each mark had been made.

Melinda had worked hard to keep the Reaper talking and Mason couldn't help the pride that he'd felt at her determination. Despite the pain he'd inflicted, Melinda still managed to keep him talking with little effort.

"Why are you doing this?" she'd asked.

"Killing you?" he wondered aloud.

"No. Mr. Donahue, the others."

"Well, Mr. Donahue was on my list already, but once I realized he knew my name, I had to reschedule our meeting. You're just collateral damage, Mel."

"That was pretty familiar," Mason commented.

"Now, Julianne...Well, she was in the first home I ended up in. It took two weeks for someone to adopt her. I spent years in foster care and she gets adopted after two weeks?" he spat.

"And Jonathon Beauford?" Melinda whispered.

"Morrow! Jon Morrow! He was my cousin. My mom's sister's kid. She died when he was little and my parents took him in for a while. But, my dad wasn't too fond of caring for someone else's kid so he forced my mom to give him up not long after he arrived. That made my mom cry."

"And the roses? Why did he have nightmares about roses?"

"Roses? Ahh, that was my father's very own brand of discipline. When we would get into trouble, he would whip us with the roses. Really quite painful."

"He whipped a three-year-old?"

"No, but it didn't stop him from whipping me in front of a three-year-old. Enough about me; let's get back to you for a moment."

Melinda's gasp was barely audible, but when he didn't speak, it was clear he'd meant getting back to her torture. After several more whimpers were detected, Melinda asked another question of the Reaper, and her voice shook with what they could only assume was pain and probably the shock settling in.

"Who were the Hartreys to you?"

Bitter laughter followed before he said, *"They were the only decent family I ever had, and then that bitch killed them."*

"Angela Forrester?"

"Yes. But, an eye for an eye. She took my family, so I took hers." The Reaper spoke gleefully.

"Who was her family?"

"The little girl who she'd been on her way to pick up. If you ask me, I did her a favor; her mother was a drunk just like my father. You haven't figured out who she was yet, have you?"

"Angela?"

"Yes. Angela. She was Cole's girl's mama."

"Was?"

"Yes, was. It was poetry. I took her at her daughter's grave that she visits every Friday."

"Where?"

"Ahh, ahh, ahh. I can't tell you everything."

"You're going to kill me, why not?"

"True."

"If you loved the Hartreys so much, why did you kill Emelie and Michael?" Melinda asked breathlessly.

"And Alyssa. Don't forget Alyssa Marchand. Because, after the accident, they had a choice, and they made the wrong one. They sent me back into the system, but they kept that little brat, Emmie. I was fifteen. Do you have any idea how difficult foster homes can be on a fifteen-year-old boy? No one wants to adopt you, and the fosters either make you their houseboy or their bitch!" he spat. *"Why should they get a happy ending when all I got was pain and suffering? They left me without so much as a second thought!"*

Melinda cried out as he undoubtedly took out his rage against her flesh.

"How many foster homes did you have?"

"Enough, I lost count after thirty. Sharing time is over!" the Reaper growled.

There was silence for a moment as water ran in the background before Melinda spoke up once more.

"You're a doctor. How can you do this?"

"It's quite easy, actually. I found that a man with my predilections could easily conceal his true nature behind the guise of a medical practitioner. Even though I don't practice medicine in the traditional sense." He laughed. *"I have access to pharmaceuticals and tools, and*

even better, I can keep tabs on the investigations without creating suspicion."

A moment later, there was a loud crash and Mason realized they had discovered how Mr. Donahue had ended up on the floor. He'd somehow manage to regain consciousness and attempted to escape as the Reaper bolted thunderously down the stairs and away from Melinda. And then, Mr. Donahue had spoken. Unfortunately, it wasn't audible over the rasp of Melinda's labored breathing, but the blood curdling scream had been clear enough as Mr. Donahue had undoubtedly been murdered in that moment.

A minute ticked by as it sounded like Melinda was struggling against restraints before the footsteps sounded on the stairs, indicating the Reaper's return. Mason knew what he was about to listen to, but it didn't make it any easier.

"You'll never get out of here without being noticed. I have an unmarked car following me."

"Ah, yes. Well, I took the liberty of introducing myself to your tail earlier. They won't be a problem. Although I should get back to them before your friend arrives. Speaking of which, I think I'd best be on my way."

The next sound they heard was the snap of plastic and the fall of weighted limbs. The Reaper had released her before he delivered what he'd planned to be the fatal blow. He could hear her struggle to stand, but it was quickly interrupted.

"Unfortunately, I just don't have the time to play. You understand, don't you?"

Those words were followed by Melinda's gasping scream of pain and the sound of useless limbs collapsing to the ground.

When Melinda's scream blared through the speakers, Mason started to pace before he said, "Again. Play it again!"

Devon nodded as he started the recording over.

Robin stood up and said, "I've already heard this a few times, if you don't mind…I'll be in the next room."

Based on what Mason saw upon finding her, he suspected that the Reaper had begun by making dozens of negligible incisions over her skin. They had been intended to instill fear and he sounded as if he had derived great joy from her discomfort. For as many wounds as he'd seen when he found her, she didn't appear to be in nearly as much pain as he would have suspected, or that she understood that he was feeding off her pain and she was attempting to deny him the satisfaction. More than likely, it was a little of both.

It appeared as though he enjoyed taking his time with his kills for the most part, almost as though the bloodletting was his way of transferring his pain to the victims; an exorcism of sorts.

They listened carefully as the Reaper spoke about his parents. He never named them, but they learned he'd been raised around some type of nursery. Mason guessed that was where the roses from Jon's nightmares came from. Unfortunately, there were hundreds of nurseries within several hours of Chicago.

The Reaper had revealed a history of abuse and the fact that he'd survived over thirty foster homes. The Hartreys had fallen somewhere in the midst of all of them.

A few leads were revealed, but nothing earth shattering was divulged.

They listened up to the point where Melinda said, "You're a doctor. How could you do this?"

Devon stopped the playback and asked, "Was that a question, or an answer?"

Mason thought for a moment as he recalled the letters she traced on his hand. "MD!" he exclaimed loudly.

Piper and Devon just stared at him, having no clue what the significance was.

"MD; they aren't initials. He's a doctor," Mason reasoned. "She wasn't asking him, she already knew. She knew him!"

Chapter 18

"She knew him?" Devon asked.

"It sure sounds like it to me," Mason stated.

"So, the question is how did she know him? And do we know him as well?" Piper wondered.

"It's certainly possible. I mean, he said he was keeping tabs on the case, but how? He didn't seem particularly nervous about her recognizing him, but then again he had no idea that she was taping the conversation or he'd have destroyed the phone," Mason offered.

"True. I don't think he had any intention of letting her live to ID him later either," Devon said.

The conversation was interrupted as Mason's phone vibrated across the counter. "This is Cole," he answered.

It was Officer Reilly, one of the officers assigned on their detail. "Lt. Commander Cole, I'm sorry to disturb you, but we just apprehended a young man trying to leave a package in the lobby with your name on it."

"Bring him in," Mason said as he headed to the elevator to wait for them.

The officer led a kid — barely out of high school, it appeared — from the elevator, carrying a small box wrapped in brown paper. Mason's name was the only marking on the box.

The kid's face was as white as a sheet. It certainly wasn't the Reaper, as he appeared on the verge of hyperventilating. The officer set the package down on the table in the conference room as he led the boy to the table where Devon and Piper were sitting.

"Who gave you this package? Did you catch a look at him?" Devon asked.

"N-n-no, sir. I-I-I w-was hanging out w-w-with my f-f-friends when a man c-c-called out to me. H-h-he told me to s-st-stay where I w-was and set the p-p-package down. H-h-he told me he'd give m-m-me t-t-two hundred d-dollars to d-deliver it t-t-to you," The kid stuttered, obviously petrified.

"Was he short, tall? Anything you can tell us would be helpful," Mason prompted as he sat down across from the kid.

"T-t-tall. Listen, man, I-I-I needed the m-money. My mom just got l-laid off and I have two kid b-b-brothers. I-I-I can't g-g-go to j-jail," he stammered in a panic.

"Look, kid, you're not going to jail. We just need to know what you saw," Mason said.

Mason turned when he heard Robin and Andy come into the room. That was when he noticed the package had begun to leak. "Stop!" Mason yelled, halting their movement.

Everyone turned towards Mason as he focused on the box. It was slightly smaller than a shoebox, but that wasn't what caught his attention. It was the dark substance that was clearly leaking from the sides of the box that had him on alert.

"Is that box bleeding?" Andy asked tentatively.

Mason held up a hand as he pulled out a pocketknife and carried the box to the table. "Dev, grab a trash bag and spread it out on the table."

Devon did as he was asked and watched as his brother set the box carefully inside the bag before he slipped the blade under the flap and popped it open.

"What is it?" Piper asked.

Mason shook his head as he pulled on a pair of gloves and looked inside the box. His expression went from curious to horrified, as he realized what sat before him. He carefully reached inside of the box, hoping what he was seeing was some kind of a joke, but as he slid his hand beneath the object, he instantly felt the warmth of the muscle and he knew he was holding the real deal. As soon as it was clearly visible, he quickly set it onto the protective bag as his throat tightened in reflex.

"Oh, God!" Devon gasped. "Is that a..."

"Get him out of here," Mason said to the officer as he pointed towards the kid.

As soon as the officer had escorted the kid back to the lobby, the rest of them moved closer to the box. Piper clapped his hand over his mouth as they stared at a human heart; still warm with a white rose protruding from what Mason believed was once the pulmonary artery, if his knowledge of anatomy still served.

The once-beautiful rose wilted under the weight of the blood that stained its petals.

"Call Hovey and get her over here, NOW!"

Piper happily took the task, which allowed him to leave the room.

"You know, she usually prefers a body attached to the internal organs," Devon stated.

"Trust me, this is her deal! She's the only person I trust to handle this," Mason answered.

Piper paced outside the door of the conference room as he waited for the doctor to answer.

"Piper, I'm not finished yet. I'll call you as soon as I am," she answered.

"Yeah, doc, that's not why I'm calling. We have a bit of a situation here and Mason wants you to take a look."

"Can it wait until morning?" she asked. "My assistant is attending his brother's funeral. He won't be back until Monday."

Mason waved to Piper who held the phone to his ear. "Doc, I know you have a lot on your plate right now, but I need you to stop what you're doing and get over here, now. Someone just delivered a human heart to the lab and it's still warm."

He heard a loud metallic scraping noise and a door slamming before she answered, "I'm on my way."

The officer took the kid down to the station with Piper to get a statement and deliver the cash he'd received to the lab. When Dr. Hovey arrived, she headed straight for Mason, stopping abruptly as she saw the box and its contents laid out in front of him.

"Oh, good lord. Someone really doesn't like you, my friend."

"You think?" Mason quipped.

"Do you have any thoughts on whose heart this is?" she asked.

"I have a guess," Mason answered.

"And?"

"Angela Forrester."

The ME nodded and looked closer at the heart. "I'm pretty sure I'll never look at a bouquet of roses the same way again," she shared as she shook her head before gently removing the rose.

"The box and the rose are all yours, but the heart is coming with me," she said as she looked at Robin and Andy.

"Will you let us know as soon as you find anything?" Devon asked.

"Obviously," she said as she shook her head at his ridiculous question.

Mason watched as the ME placed the heart into a cooler and threw her gloves along with the gloves Mason had worn into the plastic bag on which they'd set the box. "You can have these, too." She smiled as she headed for the elevator.

"I guess it's a little premature to say this, but I'm betting Angela Forrester isn't going to be found alive," Devon said.

"No, I think the Reaper just made a statement. She broke his heart, so he took hers."

"Do you think that's why his MO has started to vary?" Devon asked.

"Maybe. I think he gets off on a more disciplined approach with the ones who were in the system and seemed to have gotten the life that he desired with happy homes and supportive families. And for those he remains fairly consistent. Now, based on what we know, Angela Forrester was responsible for the Hartrey family losing their parents and he was excessively violent with Emelie Hartrey, but he didn't stray too far from his "happy place" if you will, with her brother Michael.

"Okay, so why was he so much more violent with Emelie?"

"Because her siblings raised her, but not him!" Mason exclaimed as the pieces started to fit together. "So let's backtrack here. We need to connect the dots with the kids fostered by Dakota's aunt and uncle along with the Hartreys. There might be a name that crosses over. Probably removed from his home due to violence, and I'm guessing his foster care experiences weren't much better."

"Andy and Robin, any luck uncovering anything in Donahue's files?" Devon asked.

The two of them briefed Devon as Mason stepped out into the hallway to place a couple of calls. The first was to secure a warrant based on the new evidence from the tape as well as the heart. Once that was taken care of, he dialed the offices of Children's Services and got a list of names from the two families in question; Dakota's and the Hartreys. He'd hoped for lists of all the victim's homes, but so far, they'd only been able to get the two. It was more than they had yesterday, so he'd take what he could get.

Devon continued to talk with the lab technicians about what they had been able to find. Evidently, there were a number of files that had been empty, leading them to believe that the Reaper had lifted anything that Donahue had referencing him specifically, but there was one bright spot.

It appeared that in his haste to kill Melinda, he had accidentally nicked himself at some point. There had been a third DNA profile found in the bathroom behind the radiator. It was recent, so it seemed likely he had scraped a knuckle or something while restraining Melinda in the bathroom. The sample was neither Melinda's nor Peter Donahue's.

The blood was a familial match to the third victim, Jonathon Beauford. A cousin.

Devon perked up as he remembered Peter Donahue mentioning two cousins that had been removed from the same home sometime after Jonathon was. The question was simple: which cousin were they dealing with?

Devon glanced over at his brother when he returned and said, "Any luck with the lists?"

"Maybe. There was a boy with the Hartreys. The name I found was Joseph Harlow. According to the records, the Hartreys were being evaluated to adopt the boy permanently when they died unexpectedly in that car accident. That seems like the most likely suspect, but I can't find Joseph Harlow's name listed with Dakota's family."

"That's because he wasn't there. The lab found a third DNA profile at Donahue's house. It didn't belong to Mel or Donahue, but it was fresh. So, it had to be the Reaper. And get this; it was a familial match to Jon Beauford. It's got to be one of the cousins. That's how it connects to Dakota," Devon shared.

"But then why is he after Dakota?" Mason asked.

"Maybe he's only after her because of you?" Devon supplied.

"I'm going to give Dakota a call and see if the name rings a bell," Mason said.

She picked up on the second ring, "Hey, love. How's Mel?"

"No change. The alarms aren't going off, so I'll take that as a good sign. Where are you?"

"The lab. I have a question; does the name Joseph Harlow ring a bell?"

"There used to be a rose sanctuary called Harlow-Abel Rose Sanctuary up in Racine. My mother used to take me there when I first lost my sight. She said that roses were pretty enough that you didn't have to see them to appreciate them. She always had roses; she loved them so much that she named me Dakota Rose," she answered with a bright smile as she remembered her mom.

"The owner's wife would always sit and talk to me. I think her name was Darcy. I liked her because she didn't talk to me like a lot of people did. Especially when I was little, but even today, people will talk extra loud as though my blindness also equates to being deaf or stupid. She seemed to understand though, because her oldest son, Jason, was deaf. I do remember her husband kind of had a creepy vibe, but I was still pretty young and, to be fair, when you are a kid and blind a lot of things read as creepy. I think his name was Abel like the name of the place. I remember her other son was constantly being yelled at. His name might have been Joe or Joey," she offered.

"That's a huge help, love. I'll be by to check on Melinda in about an hour. Are you okay there until then?"

"Oh, yeah. I'm fine. Molly was going to come by in an hour with lunch. Should I tell her to bring something for the three of you?"

"Just Dev and me. Piper went down to the station. We'll see you in about an hour," Mason said as he disconnected the call and followed Devon to the car.

Mason looked at his brother and smiled. Finally, a few of the pieces were starting to fall into place. At the same time, Mason's gut churned as he realized why Dakota was on the Reaper's radar. She hadn't seen him, but she did know him.

Chapter 19

"So we need to get up to Racine," Mason stated.

"Looks like that's where this is headed," Devon agreed. "I'll call Piper and check in. Then we can get back to the hospital."

Mason started to speak until his phone chirped, interrupting his train of thought. He quickly answered and placed the phone on speaker. "Cole."

"Hi, Mason, sorry to bother you," Robin said.

"No problem, we were just talking about the case anyway. Do you have something already?" he responded.

"I do."

"Well, spit it out."

"Andy ran the blood and got a DNA hit. It is Angela Forrester's."

"Okay, anything else?" Mason asked.

"Yes, are you sitting down?"

"Robin, I'm in the car. Of course I'm sitting down."

"You're not driving?" she asked.

Mason responded, sounding a little irritated, "No. I'm not driving. What's with all the concern?"

"The DNA was a familial match to another victim."

"Okay. Who?"

"Jill. According to the DNA, Angela Forrester was her mother."

"Okay, that's a lot to digest. Thanks Robin!" Devon said as he grabbed the phone and hung up.

Mason was silent for a couple of minutes before he finally spoke. "I guess we know what he meant when he said his next victim was family."

"Yeah."

"This guy's cryptic clues are really starting to piss me off," Mason said.

"I'm with you, brother."

When they arrived back at the hospital, a nurse told them where to find Dakota and Molly. They were sitting in one of the family rooms off the ICU, waiting for them to arrive.

"Hi, ladies," Devon said. "What did you bring me?"

"I brought a couple of baguettes and some chicken and wild rice soup," Molly said as Devon planted himself at her side and kissed her cheek in greeting.

Mason smiled as he watched his brother closely for a minute before he sat beside his girl and gave her a slow lingering kiss.

"I'd say get a room, but that doesn't seem to help much either," Devon quipped.

"Yeah, I'm pretty sure your day will come, big brother," Mason told him. Then he leaned over and whispered to Dakota, "Maybe sooner, rather than later."

She nodded in agreement as Mason handed her a spoon and a piece of baguette before placing her hand on the rim of her bowl.

"Thanks for this. I'm sure whatever we managed to find along the way wouldn't have been nearly as good," Devon told Molly.

"So, how's Melinda? Has the fever broken yet?" Mason asked.

"No, it's not getting any worse though," Dakota offered.

"Mind if I go check on her for a minute?"

"No. Go ahead."

Mason headed towards her room and quietly sat in the chair beside her again.

"We got a break. We heard the audio file and it helped us narrow down our suspects. His name is Joseph Harlow. We figured out where he grew up before he landed in the system, too. We're getting closer. Learning what made him into the Reaper. We're going to get him, Mel. I'm going to get him," he whispered as he kissed her forehead, instantly feeling the excessive warmth radiating off of her.

Mason stood and spotted Dakota leaning against the doorframe.

"Come to check on me?" he asked as he walked over and wrapped his arms around her.

"You're never far from my mind when I'm not with you," she whispered as she let her fingers skim over the frown that marred his perfect mouth. She couldn't see it, but she knew it was there all the same.

"You're never far from my thoughts either," he whispered as he pressed his lips softly against her temple and skimmed her hair behind her ear.

"Dakota, Dev and I need to go to Racine. Piper will stay here with you," Mason said as he tried to gauge her reaction.

"I know I can't ask you not to go, but I want to. So badly," she whispered.

"I wish there was any other way."

"Hey, you two, as much as I'd love a replay of last night, I think the nurses might take offense."

"Devon. Don't be crude," Molly chided.

"Oh, Molly. You have no idea." Dakota laughed.

They took Dakota and Molly back to the diner and waited for Piper to meet them. He arrived a few minutes after they did and they filled him in on what they'd learned, in addition to their plan to head up to Racine.

"I understand that you want someone to stick with Dakota, but don't you think that it would be best if I came with you?" Piper said.

"I do want you to come with us, but I won't put her at risk," Mason said quietly as he watched her from across the room.

"Dev, don't you have some thoughts on this?"

"Look, this guy can't come after both of us at once. If I was him and I wanted to hurt Mason, she's the one I'd target. That's all I'm saying," Devon offered.

"Okay. So, you want me to keep her here or take her to your place?"

"Whatever she wants," Mason said as he clapped him on the back and walked over to Dakota to say goodbye.

Devon looked at Piper and said, "The way I see it, you're getting the better end of the deal. I get to spend an hour each way in the car after I spent all of last night listening to those two trying to be quiet. And let me tell you, they suck at it. So think of me having awkward conversations with Mase all the way to Wisconsin."

Mason returned and looked between the pair of them, smirking as he walked out to the car. "Let's get out of here, Dev."

The ride was uneventful apart from the construction on 94 that bottlenecked traffic near the border. Devon had managed to keep quiet for most of the trip, but as they sat motionless on the highway, he needed something to pass the time.

"So, want to talk about it?"

"About what?" Mason asked as he stared out the window.

"I don't know. Dakota maybe?"

"No. Not really. How about we talk about Molly?" Mason offered.

"Nothing to talk about. You and Dakota on the other hand, oh, yes. Lots to talk about there, little brother."

"Look, I don't think you heard anything I haven't heard before."

"Oh, see that's where I beg to differ. Sleeping in the next room was like watching The Notebook with your mom."

"Hey, you could have slept in the basement bedroom. No one said you had to stay upstairs. Or there's always oh, I don't know, your house?"

Fortunately, traffic started to move once again and Mason dialed the Racine Police Department to get an escort out to the property. They weren't planning to take any chances, and they were pushing their luck on jurisdiction. The only reason they were able to get on the property without a warrant was that it was open to the public. But, at least the local PD was willing to work with them based on the information they had provided earlier that morning. Things would go a lot smoother with back up.

When they arrived, they didn't expect to see a rusted out chain across the drive with a closed sign hanging off of it.

"It's normally open seven days a week," one of the officers stated. "We'll head up and see if anyone is around."

Mason and Devon sat in their car at the end of the drive. One of the other teams removed the chain and headed up closer to the nearest building.

A few minutes later, the police radio blared, "No one appears to be on the property, but it's open."

The other two teams drove up towards the main building and they followed. Mason had an uneasy feeling as he stepped from the passenger seat, but he decided it was simply because he'd been hoping the Reaper might have enough of an ego to face them, knowing they didn't quite have enough to hold him on. Yet.

There were four teams of two in total. Mason and Devon moved quickly through what looked like a barn, finding nothing out of place as they headed for the large greenhouse towards the back of the property.

When they got to the main doors, Mason noticed an odd coloration on one of the panes of glass towards the back of the structure.

"What is that?" Mason wondered.

"Not sure. Dirt maybe?" Devon offered.

Mason radioed to the other teams that they were entering the greenhouse before he reached for the door. As it swung open, he was hit with a cloud of putrid, damp air. He knew whatever lay beyond the doors was not living.

Devon coughed as he called back to the other teams, alerting them to the distinct odor of decomposing flesh.

Mason pulled his shirt up over his nose and mouth as he moved further into the greenhouse. The closer they got to the discolored pane of glass, the more vile the smell became.

Devon hung back as the radio crackled, but Mason continued to creep forward, taking in the space around him. He was certain that the Reaper was finished with this place, the further he got. When he turned back and noticed his brother was no longer visible, he called out. "Dev?"

"Right behind you. Just give me a sec," he shouted in response.

Mason finally made it into the clearing near the back of the greenhouse when he saw what had created such a horrendous stench. Two bodies stretched out on the two tables in the center of the room. One was a young woman who looked emaciated and scarred. She'd been subjected to rounds of torture and bloodletting; her only recent wound was a precise ribbon-like cut carved from the lobe of one ear to the other. Her eyes were sunken and clouded after several days of decomposition.

173

The male had a healthier appearance; he didn't look like he'd been tortured or starved, but he'd been murdered nonetheless. What stood out about him was that his mouth had been sewn shut, ante mortem based on the appearance of blood surrounding each suture. Afterwards, he'd been bled to death in a similar manner to the Reaper's prior victims. His arms had been secured over his head and it was now clear that the marks on the pane had been dried blood, as he had not been forced to bleed slowly; the Reaper's only mercy having been a quick death for this particular victim.

He clutched a photograph in his hand. It showed two young boys holding their mother's hand and their father standing beside them. On the back was written, "Abel and Darcy Harlow with Jason and Joseph Harlow." And finally, there was a message, which had been carefully written in blood across the male victim's chest.

Silent in life, silent in death.

"Well that's dark." Mason said to himself.

As Mason crept closer to the male victim, he heard his brother and two of the local PD officers round the corner.

"Oh, holy crap. Could have given us a little warning, Mase," Devon said as he stared at the macabre scene before him.

"Preoccupied," Mason answered as he reached out with a gloved hand and turned the male victim's head to the side.

"Meet Jason Harlow," he stated.

"How can you tell?"

"Cochlear implants. Based on the message, I'd say Joseph Harlow blamed his big brother for not protecting him. Clearly, everyone on this property had to have been aware of the beatings based on what the Reaper told Melinda. So, maybe he thought brother dearest should have spoken up?" Mason posited.

"So who's the girl? He really didn't like her," Devon said as he looked at all of the healed wounds.

"Not sure, but based on what we've learned and who he seems to blame directly…Maybe Alyssa Marchand?" Mason thought aloud.

"She was the half sister of two of his earlier victims. Seems like she's one of the people he blames for his unhappy existence.

She and her brother decided to care for their young sister when their parents died, but they let Joseph go back in to foster care. He'd considered them his family and that betrayal was something he carried with him," Devon told the officers that had accompanied him.

"Well, I think it's safe to say he's exacted his revenge on her," one of the officers said.

Mason walked back out into the fresh air while the other teams descended on the greenhouse. He pulled his phone from his pocket and dialed Dr. Hovey. He was certain she wasn't going to be happy about having to drive up to Wisconsin, given that her assistant was out of town.

"Hello, Mason. Please tell me that you have not got more work for me," she said.

"Dr. Hovey, there is nothing I would love to do more than tell you we've caught the Reaper and you can take a vacation, but you and I both know that's not what this call is about."

"Where?" she said with a sigh.

"Racine."

"Wisconsin?" she wailed.

"Sorry, doc, but you and I both know you wouldn't be happy with another ME handling this."

"No. I wouldn't," she answered. "I'll leave as soon as I can."

Mason put his phone back in his pocket as Devon stepped out into the frigid, but fresh air. "I take it the good doctor was not thrilled with our excursion?"

He shook his head. "Nope. Not at all."

Chapter 20

Dakota had asked Piper to take her to the hospital to sit with Melinda. He'd agreed only because he needed to take care of a couple of things, and he knew it was the safest place. He'd gotten several calls from the lab regarding several key pieces of evidence, but he hadn't wanted to drag her along.

"I'll be back in an hour or so. Just do me a favor and don't go anywhere without taking one of the officers with you, all right?"

"Piper, I'm not going anywhere. I just don't think she should be alone," she said as he patted her shoulder and headed out to check on the evidence.

Melinda's fever had broken earlier that afternoon, so the doctors had decided to lighten up her sedation. Dakota was hopeful that Melinda was more cognizant of her surroundings and that maybe hearing a familiar voice would help her in some way.

She spoke about Devon and Molly for a bit, laughing to herself as she recalled how hard Devon was fighting against his own feelings. She thought that for a sighted man, he sure couldn't see what was standing right in front of him. And of course, she could. And it made her happy, since Molly was one of her closest friends and Devon was quickly becoming an important part of her life, too.

Sometime later, Dakota heard a gentle knock on the door.

"Good evening, I didn't mean to disturb you. I just need to check Ms. Kade's vitals. Do feel free to keep talking if you like. I'm certain that she can hear you," a soft male voice said.

Dakota smiled as she spoke. "I tried to tell our friend that, but he thinks it's silly."

"Ah yes. Detective Torello. Well, I think he's just having a hard time accepting his friend's condition. He'll come around." The man spoke in a gentle voice.

"You know Piper?" she asked.

"We met in the hall earlier," he said.

"Oh, I didn't think he was going to be back for a while," she said.

"I think he might have been heading out, actually."

"Are there any changes?" Dakota asked.

"Well, she seems to be doing remarkably well considering everything I put her through," the man said, this time with considerably more venom in his voice.

"Pardon me?" Dakota asked, confused.

"I'm terribly sorry; I forgot to introduce myself. You might remember me as Joseph Harlow," he said as he walked over to her side and clutched her elbow quite painfully, before clasping a hand firmly over her mouth. "Now. Here's what's going to happen. You are going to put your arm through mine and follow me. We're going to tell the officers that I am taking you down to the cafeteria for a cup of coffee and discuss Ms. Kade's case and that I will return you in no time. If you behave, I will call them and tell them what the little cocktail was that I just slipped to Melinda so that they can save her. If you don't, then she will die and her blood will be on your hands. Understood?" he whispered, holding her arm in a death grip.

"Yes. I understand," she said very calmly.

A few moments later, the two of them walked out into the hallway, only to be stopped by the officers. Dakota felt the hard grasp of his fingers at her elbow as they spoke to her.

"Miss Shelton, Officer Torello instructed that one of us should stay with you at all times."

"Oh, it's okay. The doctor was just going to accompany me to the cafeteria for a cup of coffee while he tells me about Melinda's progress. We'll be back in ten minutes," she said, hoping that they couldn't see her pulse pounding away at her throat.

"I promise to have her back well before Piper returns," The officers seemed to relax at the doctor's use of his first name.

She felt his grip tighten as he led her away and she listened intently for any kind of sign that Melinda was in distress.

"That was very good. I almost would have believed you myself," he sneered.

After a few minutes, she realized that they were in an elevator. When the doors opened, cold air assailed her and she knew they were leaving the hospital. Her heart began to pound frantically as the darkness that was always surrounding her became even more foreboding.

She had no idea if there were other people around. She could smell gas fumes, so she assumed they were in the parking garage, but she had no way of knowing if there would be anyone to hear her if she screamed. If there wasn't, she most certainly would not survive long enough for anyone to even be aware that she was gone.

Her tears fell like icicles in the cold winter air.

"I went with you. Now call them and tell them about Melinda," she said as she halted her movement.

"Now, now. We are still on the property. I can't risk tipping them off before we've made our escape," he whispered as he forcibly began to drag her, all but confirming that there were no witnesses in that garage.

"What do you want with me?" she said as her tears continued to flow.

"You? Nothing. I just want to have a little sit down with your boyfriend. I figured you would be the fastest way to get him alone."

"Why? What is he to you?" she said as she pulled against him.

"Well, he's the reason I've had to work so hard. The irony is, this will end the same way it started. With the woman he loves."

"Please don't hurt him," she pleaded.

"Oh, I won't," he answered. "I'm just going to hurt you. He'll be collateral damage."

A moment later, she felt a burning sensation in her neck and felt the ground move sideways beneath her feet.

Devon and Mason were sitting in the car at the end of the drive when Dr. Hovey arrived.

"What the hell is this place?" Dr. Hovey asked as she looked around at the now darkened drive.

"Harlow-Abel Rose Sanctuary," Mason said.

"Only it's not the happy place Dakota remembers from when she was a kid," Devon shared.

"What do you mean? How does Dakota fit into this whole picture?" she asked, waving her hands towards what appeared to be a rundown nursery.

"Her mom used to bring her here when she was little," Mason offered.

"Well, that's an odd coincidence," she stated.

"There are a few of those. Like Jon Beauford used to live here before he was placed with Dakota's aunt and uncle until he was adopted," Mason told her.

"So, what led you here?" she asked.

"Dakota recognized the name and remembered this place. Though I'll admit, we thought we were coming to a functioning business, not some desolate frozen tomb for his older brother."

"That bad? Maybe we should go and take a look, then," Dr. Hovey said as she asked him to lead the way.

Mason never could understand how the ME could walk into something that smelled so foul and did not even turn up her nose. He chalked it up to occupational hazard, but he knew he would never get used to the things that he'd seen recently. No more than he could get used to the horrible things he'd witnessed as a SEAL.

The local PD had been working diligently to get the juvenile records for the Harlow's children, including adoption and foster care records. Devon made a call to their precinct to alert them to the situation they'd happened upon. He spoke to Detective Laue of the Racine PD while Mason and Dr. Hovey went into the greenhouse.

The detective told Devon that he'd been called out to the property a number of times when the children were young. He'd been green at the time, just out of the academy, but he remembered the family well.

He also mentioned that there were a number of reports from the ER and the boys' teachers regarding possible cases of abuse before the boys were finally removed from the home.

The detective had the case files and photos emailed to Devon, who flipped through them on his tablet. He was becoming acutely aware of what had caused Jon Beauford's nightmares when he was a child.

The first report indicated that Jon Morrow entered into the system a year after being placed with the Harlows by Lauren Morrow after she succumbed to cancer. She had been Darcy Harlow's sister.

He opened the second file, and what he found was beyond disturbing. The file showed photos of a young child, Joseph Harlow, with numerous lashes and punctures that had become infected. The initial reports stated that he'd fallen into a rose bush, but the ER physician stated that the injuries were more likely caused by being hit repeatedly with long, barbed objects. Based on the resultant infection, they assumed the long barbed objects had been long-stemmed roses.

The third file indicated Jon Morrow had been placed in foster care due to the family's financial woes. And as he looked at the next file, Devon realized he'd ended up with a far better circumstance than the one he'd left.

As the next file indicated, Joseph returned to the hospital a month later with similar injuries, indicated by a second report that was filed with the Racine Department of Child Protective Services. His brother Jason had been removed as well when they'd discovered evidence that his hearing loss was due to a skull fracture that occurred when he was a toddler. Devon was starting to think there was some truth to Mason's theory, but it appeared that Jason might not have been any better off.

Dr. Hovey looked over both victims. She was certain that the female victim had been held for a substantial amount of time, based on her emaciated state and the various stages of healing she'd seen in the wounds.

"She's been held for at least a number of months, possibly longer," she said absently.

When she walked over to the male victim, she stopped in her tracks. She quickly turned his head to the side and took note of his hearing devices. Then she looked more closely at his facial features.

"Everything okay, doc?"

"Oh, God," Dr. Hovey gasped as she glanced at the photograph.

"What? What is it?" Mason asked.

"The Reaper uses near surgical precision..." Dr. Hovey said, lost in thought.

"Yeah, Melinda kept tracing MD on my hand. I thought it was initials, but then we heard the tape. She called him a doctor," Mason offered.

"That's because he is one. Abel and Darcy," she said as though she was thinking out loud.

"Yes, we've established that," Mason said, trying to figure out where she was headed.

"I know who the Reaper is."

"What?" Devon shouted from the front of the greenhouse as he made his way to them at a sprint.

"It's Joe."

"Who?" Devon asked.

"My assistant, Joseph Darcy. Abel and Darcy Harlow," she said as she started to search her phone frantically.

"Oh, God, it is! His middle name is Abel!" Dr. Hovey shouted upon finding what she was looking for.

"Where is he now?" Mason yelled.

"His brother's funeral!" she screamed as she pointed to the male victim.

"Son of a bitch!" Mason said as he ran towards his brother. "Dev, get Piper on the phone. The Reaper is Hovey's assistant!"

Devon frantically searched his pockets for his phone just as Mason's began to ring.

"Piper, we were just about to call you!" he answered.

"Mason, I'm so sorry. I left her with two officers. They said she went to the cafeteria with Melinda's doctor," Piper said frantically.

"What are you talking about? I was calling to tell you we know who the Reaper is."

"He has her, Mase. He has Dakota!"

"Who does?"

"The Reaper!" Piper answered.

Mason's heart started to race as he choked on his next breath. "How long, Piper?"

"Twenty minutes, maybe." Mason could hear a code being called on the monitors, alerting him to the fact that Piper was still at the hospital.

"Call Taber and get everyone you can looking for her. Security footage, personnel documents, everything. You're looking for Joe Darcy."

"Hovey's assistant?"

"Yes. He's the Reaper!" Mason shouted as he hung up the phone.

Mason pointed to Devon. "Drive. He's got her, Dev. He's got Dakota."

Chapter 21

Dakota began to wake up. Her limbs felt heavy like they were asleep or something. She was surrounded by silence as she tried to hone in on any sounds to indicate if she was alone, or perhaps where she was. But she heard nothing more than traffic and a siren off in the distance. In a city like Chicago, that wasn't very helpful.

She wiggled her fingers, only to find she'd been left untied. Clearly, he was confident that her vision impairment was enough to give him the upper hand, or he was certain she could not escape the room in which he'd left her. At this point, she was willing to try, though.

She pushed away from the chair she'd been sitting on, only to crumple to the floor. Her legs felt weightless beneath her. Whatever he'd given her clearly wasn't going to make escaping any easier.

She felt her throat burn with fear when she heard footsteps coming towards her.

"Such a brave little thing. It would be a shame to see you injured prematurely," he said with humor in his tone.

"What do you want?" she asked.

"Simple, really. I want Lt. Commander Cole to swoop in to save you, only to watch you die."

"Why?" she asked.

"Because. He made me what I am today. He kept me from getting what I needed all that time ago. Instead, I had to hunt down each lead. You see, he and I aren't that different. We both seek answers. We both want to put an end to the injustices of the world. Only my reasons are just a bit more self-serving," he answered.

"Who are you trying to save?" she asked.

"Why, me of course," he whispered in her ear, causing her to flinch away from him.

"You think you're the only kid that survived an abusive guardian?" she spat.

"The only one I care about. And you see, I'm done. Everyone has paid for their transgressions," he said as he yanked her arm and tossed her back into the chair.

"Then why Mason? Or me? Why not just be on your way, then?"

"See, Mason is going to kill me for what I've done to you. And it will all finally be over. But, I want him to remember me. This could have ended a year ago. She was just about to tell me where to find Mommy Dearest and then her Navy SEAL had to come home. I was forced to stop short of my goal. See, she didn't have to die if she'd just answered my question. None of them did. And it's all his fault. If only I'd had two more minutes with Jill, I could have found Angela and it could have ended there. When she died, the others became a necessity, but then...then I started to have fun! He didn't have to keep looking for me, but he just couldn't let go."

"If you want to die, there are lots of ways to ensure that happens. You don't need him to kill you."

"No, but it just seems so poetic. At the end of the day, we're both killers. He just stands on the right side of the law," he told her.

Piper had found surveillance footage from the garage of Dakota and Dr. Hovey's assistant. He'd been wearing scrubs and a lab coat, so no one had questioned his presence as he'd left with her.

He'd also found him on a number of traffic cams heading out towards Wells and North Avenue. He'd parked on a side street off of Wells that had a number of clubs with lots of people milling about, so that was as far as Piper could track them.

As Piper was searching for them, his phone rang. It was Mason.

"How far are you?" Piper asked.

"About twenty minutes. Do you have any idea where he took her?"

"North and Wells. That's as far as I could track them. He parked on a side street. There were a lot of people walking from bar to bar. I lost them," Piper said.

186

"What's the name of the side street?"

"Schiller," Piper answered.

"Dev, I know where he's taken her!" He yelled.

"Jill's."

"Piper, get to 1300 N Wells. Unit 3B. We'll be there soon. Don't move on him. He wants me; he's going to get me," Mason said as his heart raced violently.

"On my way," Piper said as he hung up.

"Mase, you really think it's a good idea to go in there alone?"

"I'm not," he said as he pulled a lock pick set from his coat pocket and held it up for Devon to see.

Fifteen minutes later, they pulled up at the corner of Wells and North and ran down the block to where Piper was waiting.

"I'm going up. He's expecting me to come, but I'm going to try and get a look inside before I go in," Mason said to the two of them.

Devon nodded, hoping that his brother had a plan that didn't involve anyone getting shot at, least of all Dakota. Devon knew the guy already had a very slim chance of walking out of that building, but he was hoping the only shots fired came from them.

A few minutes after he'd watched his brother enter the building, his phone rang.

"I'm on the 4th floor fire escape. I have a pretty good view of the unit from here," Mason whispered.

"What do you see?"

"He's inside with Dakota. She's in the living room and he's closer to the front door, near the kitchen. Dev, I need you to do me a favor."

Devon never liked the favors his brother asked of him; they usually ended up with someone getting shot at, but he couldn't say no. "What do you need, Mase?"

"Get into the hallway as quietly as possible. He can't know you're there. Listen carefully. When you hear the phone ring, you need to keep him focused on the front door. Whatever you do, he needs to believe I'm on my way," Mason said.

"Okay, but you better not take long to get up there; something tells me he's not going to be reasonable," Devon said as the call disconnected.

He turned to Piper and said, "I hate this. I just want to go on record that if my brother gets me killed, I'm going to haunt his ass for eternity."

Piper shook his head and followed Devon up the stairs. They'd managed to get keys to the unit across the hall, so they sent a female officer in street clothes to that door to mask their movements.

Mason dialed his phone quickly as he sat on the fire escape above where Dakota sat.

Dr. Hovey answered on the first ring. "What's going on?"

"I need you to call him. Grab a phone from one of the officers, anyone. When I say," Mason said, knowing that if that phone didn't ring, he was going to have to go to plan B, which he didn't really have.

She listened intently, hearing him breathing. A moment later, she heard Mason whisper, "Go."

Devon and Piper were waiting for a signal, when they heard the shrill sound of a cell phone. They were hoping that was what they were waiting for and that Mason had some grand plan already set in motion.

"Hey, Joe. Why don't you open the door!" Devon bellowed as he crouched down to the right of the doorframe. A second later, a shot was fired through the front door.

"I told you we were going to get shot at!" he whispered to Piper, who was safely on the other side of the doorframe.

"Either Mason comes in here alone, or I shoot the girl," the Reaper yelled back towards the hole he'd shot through the door.

"He's on his way. He went looking for you in Racine."

"He'd better hurry, or he's going to see history repeating when he finds her blood painting these walls again!"

"If you hurt her, one of us will get a shot off!" Devon yelled.

"That won't matter; she'll already be dead, and he'll go back to being the broken man he was a year ago."

Devon looked at Piper and whispered, "What's he doing? He better hope this guy doesn't lose his patience first!"

"Tell Mason he's got five, four, three, two…"

A fraction of a second later, Dakota heard a click behind them.

"One," Mason whispered, the sound of the safety registered with the Reaper just as the bullet pierced the back of his skull and he dropped to the ground in a heap.

Mason's hand closed over Dakota's bicep as he pulled her back into his arms and whispered, "I've got you. You're safe now."

The front door burst open as Piper and Devon moved towards them, kicking the gun off to the side as a number of officers came running out of the stairwell, relief clear on both of their faces as they made eye contact with a fierce-looking Mason Cole. Devon knew the biggest mistake this guy had ever made was threatening Dakota and hurting Mel. The predator in Mason had come to life the moment the Reaper laid a hand on Dakota.

She shook violently as the adrenaline drained from her system, but Mason just held on tighter and crooned reassurances until she finally threw her arms around his neck and let the tears fall.

"I'm right here, love. I'm not going anywhere," Mason whispered as he kissed her forehead and held her a little tighter.

"A little warning on the plan would have been great, Superspy," Devon quipped.

"If I'd told you what I was planning, you would never have let me do it," he said as he lifted Dakota into his arms and carried her into the hallway towards the elevator. "Besides, I wasn't sure I could get the back door open without him hearing me, but the shot he fired at you was pretty convenient."

"Awesome, he shoots at us and you think that's a good thing."

"You can yell at me when my plan doesn't work, but this was a win."

"What about Melinda? He said he drugged her!" Dakota shouted in a panic.

Piper put a hand on her arm and said, "She's fine, Dakota. The doctors checked her as soon as they realized you were gone. Her vitals were a little sluggish so they amped up her fluids and gave her atropine to counteract the effect of the drugs in her system."

Mason glared at him. "Speaking of sharing the plan. Come on, man!"

Piper just said, "Need to know. I needed you focused on Dakota. Melinda was already being taken care of."

When they got to the ground level, Mason set Dakota down on the gurney in the ambulance and told Devon to sit with her. "I'll be right back."

He handed his gun to Commander Taber. "Sir, I fired one round."

"He's dead?" Taber asked.

Mason nodded. "If you don't mind, I'm going to take Dakota to the hospital to get her checked out."

"We'll need statements," Taber said.

"Tomorrow. You'll get them tomorrow," he said as he headed back to Dakota.

Dakota felt the ambulance shift as Mason climbed in and pulled her into his arms. He closed his eyes and listened to her slow, easy breaths as she leaned into his embrace. Relief flooded through his veins.

When they finally got to the hospital, the doctors ran a full blood workup and IV fluids just to be sure any drugs had been flushed from her system.

Piper came by and took the evidence bag with their clothing back to the lab, so for the second time this week Mason was stuck in a pair of scrubs. He couldn't complain, though, because Dakota was safe in his arms and the Reaper was dead.

Once the doctors were satisfied that Dakota wasn't going to need to stay overnight, Mason took her up to the ICU. The nurses came rushing over to greet them and told them they could both go in to see Melinda.

When they walked around the corner, Dakota heard a very soft voice say, "I heard you slayed the dragon and saved the girl."

"Turns out he should have stuck with the scalpel," Mason said as he led Dakota to her bedside.

Melinda reached out, grasped Dakota's hand, and said, "I heard you saved my life."

"Me? No," she answered.

"Actually, you did. The audio on the surveillance tape caught you arguing with the man who took you about saving your friend here," the nurse said as she came into the room. "We were able to get fluids and atropine into her system before she crashed."

Mason kissed Dakota on the forehead before doing the same to Melinda. "I've never been so scared in my life as I was when I found you, Melinda. Until tonight, that is."

"Could have fooled me," Devon said as he walked in and gave Melinda a kiss. "Never been so glad to see you in my life."

"You guys aren't looking so bad yourselves," she answered.

Mason could feel Dakota leaning further into his arms. The adrenaline was fading fast and all he wanted to do was get her home.

"Dev, would you mind giving us a ride home?"

"No problem. We'll be back in the morning, Mel," Devon said as he rubbed the back of her hand.

"Love you guys," Melinda said as she closed her eyes.

Mason opened the front door and said, "You staying here tonight?" to his brother.

"Yeah. If that's okay with you."

"Basement," Mason said as he carried Dakota upstairs to get cleaned up. He'd have easily just fallen into bed were it not for their close proximity to a gunshot victim.

Mason set Dakota on the side of the bathtub as he turned on the water and added a scoop of bath salts to the water.

After he helped her undress, he stepped over the edge and lifted her to stand in front of him before settling into the warm water. Within minutes, she was nearly asleep against his chest as he gently washed her hair and ran a washcloth over her skin. By the time he'd rinsed all the soap from their skin, she was barely awake.

"Are you ready to go to sleep?" he asked her.

She smiled up at him and said, "I am, but I'm starving."

Mason kissed her as he wrapped his flannel bathrobe around her and led her back into the bedroom, only to find a tray sitting in the middle of the bed with a domed lid and a roaring fire in the fireplace.

"Looks like you have some pretty amazing friends who don't mind having my brother as an accomplice," he whispered as he pulled her up onto his lap and removed the lid, revealing a giant Belgian waffle with fresh strawberries and whipped cream.

She smelled the strawberries as soon as he lifted the lid. "Molly." She smiled.

When they finished the waffle, Mason took the tray down to the kitchen. He smiled when he found Devon asleep on his couch with Molly sleeping beside him. As he crept back into the bedroom, he closed the door and crawled into bed, wrapping his arms around Dakota.

"Thank you," she whispered.

"For what?"

"Saving me?"

"There was never any other option. I told you I wouldn't lose you, and I meant it," he said as kissed her softly.

"I'm glad you did, because I love you, Mase," she whispered.

"Dakota, you may not know it…but you saved me. I would have spent the rest of my life chasing darkness if you hadn't come into my life, and I love you, too," he said as he pulled her into his arms and kissed her forehead, then closed his eyes and finally let the stress fall away.

Epilogue

It had been a month since the Reaper had finally been put in the ground. Angela Forrester's body had been recovered from an old crypt a few yards away from Jill's grave and been laid to rest beside her daughter. And Melinda was being released from the hospital in a few days, and while the road to recovery was still going to take some time, she was getting stronger every day.

Everything was falling into place.

Mason smiled because he had just gotten a call from his brother regarding a piece of unfinished business he'd been hoping to take care of.

He casually walked into the diner and glanced over at the counter where Devon had been chatting with Molly. As soon as she'd spotted him, she pointed discreetly towards the table near the kitchen with a scowl.

Devon leaned over and kissed her cheek before he followed his brother and sat across from the man while Mason sat down right beside him.

"Excuse me, but there are a dozen other tables for you gentlemen to sit at," the man snarled.

"Oh, I know. But, I really wanted to have a chat with you, Mr. Hagen," Mason said as he wrapped his hand firmly around the back of the older man's neck.

"Get your hands off of me before I have my niece call the cops!" he bellowed.

He glanced around, feeling a bit uneasy as he realized they were the only patrons in the diner at the moment.

"Molly, would you mind calling the cops for this man?" Devon called out. "Aw, never mind, sweetheart, I forgot...We are the cops." Devon smiled as both he and Mason slammed their badges down on the table.

The man cowered slightly as Mason tightened his grip on his neck and leaned in to the man to say, "Now, I thought I would take a minute to introduce myself. I'm Lieutenant Commander

Mason Cole, and this is my brother Detective Devon Cole. Seeing as we're going to be family, I thought I owed it to you to have a chat with you about your niece, Dakota."

"W-what? Family?" Gerald Hagen asked.

"Yes, you see, I've got a ring burning a hole in my pocket right now, and I intend to put that ring on Dakota's finger very soon."

"You can't be serious! That girl doesn't need a husband; she needs a caretaker," he snarled.

Mason slammed his fist down on the table, startling Gerald and the girls behind the counter.

Devon snickered as he watched Mason turn on the older man, his voice measured, but full of venom.

"You would do well to remember that Dakota is far more capable than you are, you lecherous piece of shit. You preyed on her because it made you feel stronger, but I'm here to remind you that you are weak! If you set foot anywhere near Dakota, or any of these lovely ladies that work here, you and I will not be having a polite conversation. I will bury you so deep in the bowels of the worst prison I can land you in and you can take a turn as the prey. I assure you they will not initiate you gently. You are not to speak to her, or pop in for a visit under any circumstances, unless she contacts you," Mason growled.

"Which, between you and me....Never going to happen," Devon said conspiratorially as he pointed between himself and the older man.

"Are we clear?" Mason asked in his most polite tone.

"Yes, Mason." Gerald jumped in his seat as Mason slammed his fist down on the table again. "I mean, Lieutenant Commander Cole," he stammered.

"Excellent. I'm so glad that we could have this conversation," Mason said once again in a polite tone as he clapped him on the back. "Now, let me escort you to your car."

"No, really, that's not necessary," the man said with fear clearly marring his features.

"I insist. I just need to take down your plate number, make, and model. Next time any cop sees your car within a hundred yards of Dakota's home or place of business, I'll know about it," he said as he slapped him hard on the back and led him out to his car.

Once the door closed, the girls stood behind the counter and stared at the doorway that had concealed Dakota during their conversation.

As she stepped out, they all tried to gauge her reaction. She stood stock still in silence until she heard Mason come back into the diner.

"I think he was sufficiently intimidated," Mason whispered against her neck as he wrapped his arms around her.

"You think?" Devon said as he pointed to the booth they'd recently vacated. "Clean up on aisle three. Looks like your boyfriend scared the piss out of Uncle Gerald."

With that, the entire room filled with peals of laughter.

"Well, that ought to make for an uncomfortable ride home," Dakota said as she leaned up and kissed Mason on the lips, and then wrapped her arms around Devon and kissed his cheek.

"Thank you," she whispered.

"Don't thank me, sweetheart, thank bad cop over there. He's a pro at that." Devon laughed.

"It was kind of hot," Dakota said, wrapping her arms around Mason once more.

"Totally," came a chorus from the ladies behind the counter.

"You can't really do all those things you threatened, can you?" Judy asked.

"What matters is that he thinks that I can, but for the record, if he bothers any of you again...I'll do my best to make good on every single threat. One phone call, ladies, if ANYONE ever bothers you," he said. "Day or night."

"Did I tell you he was a good one, or what?" Judy said from across the room.

"She did, you know. The first night you came in, she told me you were nursing a broken heart, but that it was solid gold," Dakota told him.

Mason ran his fingers through Dakota's hair and then walked over to Judy and kissed her on the cheek. "Thanks for seeing past the broken man and helping me find my way to be worthy of the only woman who could put the pieces back together."

"You are a good man, and no one deserves you more than that pretty girl over there," she whispered as she pushed him back towards Dakota.

"Well, if you don't mind, I'm going to steal this beautiful woman away from you. We've got a date," he said as he nudged her elbow with his and waited for her to take a hold before they took a walk in the brisk spring air and headed home.

"So where are you taking me?" she asked.

"We're going on our first date, again," he whispered.

"As first dates go, I think it's definitely worth re-visiting." She smiled.

"I'm glad you think so."

When they got home, he took her up to their room and started a bubble bath for her. He kissed her cheek and told her, "There's a box on the table in the closet for you. If you need anything, just call. I'm going to get dinner started."

She smiled as she comfortably made her way into their closet unassisted and slid the top off the box. Her hands ran across the softest cashmere sweater dress, a pair of cotton leggings and smooth silk undergarments. She smiled as she felt the supple leather of her favorite pair of boots laid out beside the box.

She turned back towards the bath with the smile still lingering as she peeled her clothes off and settled into the warm bath just moments before she heard Mason's soft footsteps on the carpet outside the door, followed by a song that always made her think of Mason.

"You know I'm going to find a way to let you have your way with me,

You know I'm going to find the time to catch your hand and make you stay.

I don't care what clothes you wear, it's time to love, and I don't care."

~ "Find A Way" by SafetySuit

"I came to bring you something to drink," he whispered. "It's right here; just reach forward a little."

When she did as he asked, he slid into the water behind her and whispered, "Never mind, I think I'd rather hold this for you."

Mason lifted the glass to her lips and let her take a sip of the champagne. When a little escaped down her chin, Mason set the glass on the ledge and chased the drops that clung to her skin with his tongue.

"I thought you were making dinner," she purred.

"I was, but I found something far more tempting right here," he whispered against her collarbone.

It was more than an hour later before they'd had dinner and Mason had led Dakota up to the rooftop, the space heaters keeping them warm as he told her how bright the stars were. He held her close and they swayed to the soft music that played in the distance.

"You know the clarity of the sky and the moon are perfect, but there is only one thing that would make this date even better than our last first date," he whispered.

"What's that? Because the last one was pretty memorable." She smiled as her hands coasted over the soft cotton of his shirt, gliding over the hard planes of his chest.

"It would definitely be better if you would make me one promise."

"Anything," she agreed.

"Promise me that this will be the last first date you'll ever have," he whispered as he took a half step away from her.

Confusion dawned on her face momentarily, until she felt the warmth of his hand on hers and the brush of his lips on her knuckles as he whispered, "Marry me."

The words stole her breath away as she felt him get down on one knee, sliding a cool band over her ring finger and kissing her knuckle again before he smoothed her right index finger across the surface of the band. She smiled as she recognized one simple word in Braille.

Always

A tear slipped down her cheek as she knelt down in front of him and whispered breathlessly, "Yes."

Before she finished that breath, she felt Mason's lips press firmly against hers as his fingers threaded into her hair.

He pulled away and whispered, "This is the best last first date ever." Then, his lips found hers once again.

She could feel the smile on his lips as she replied, "I can think of a way to make it better."

"Mmmm. I'm listening," he said as she whispered, "I was thinking about maybe taking bad cop to bed."

Seconds later, she landed on the chaise surrounded by a down comforter, the man that she loved, and the most perfect starlit sky she never saw....

Excerpt from: The Blue Line Bone Collector

From Kristi Loucks' exciting "Chicago Serial Crimes," Book Two

It had been unseasonably warm for early February in Chicago, but at two o'clock in the morning, the streets were still relatively quiet in Logan Square. Having lived in the city most of her life, Molly Shaw was no stranger to public transportation and she was always aware of what was happening around her.

She had just moved through the turnstile at the "El" station and she was headed towards the steps to the platform, when she noticed a tall thin man lurking in the shadows at the top of the landing. Her instincts put her on edge as she tried to get a read on him before ultimately turning back towards the street behind her. She could feel the rumble of the "El" as it coasted into the station above them, and she prayed that the man would be lured towards the train.

As she made it back to the turnstiles, she chanced a look back in the direction of the stairs. When she didn't see the man, she breathed a sigh of relief while she berated herself for her evident paranoia. Her relief was short lived. When she turned back toward the exit, Molly caught a glimpse of the man as he reached out from her right side.

She gasped as she saw the glint of a steel blade and tried to scream as his hand clamped over her mouth, just before the blade tore through her skin.

"Such lovely bone structure," he whispered, staring at the blood that coated her skin and running his thumb over the bones of her wrist.

Molly was fixated on the blood that ran in thin rivulets across the veins protruding from the back on her hand. That was when she noticed the markings that covered the hand of the man who held her captive.

Though she was spared further contemplation of those markings when pain shot through her system. Molly cried out behind his hand, which reeked of bleach and cigarettes, as she heard the sickening crackle and pop of bone and ligaments when he savagely wrenched her arm back at an awkward angle. In an instant, her survival instincts kicked into high gear, briefly drowning out the pain.

She fought hard as he pulled her back towards the shadows from which he'd emerged, slamming her forehead against the rail as she struggled against him. She could feel the warmth of her blood as it ran down her temple. She frantically dug through her bag, which hung to her left side, looking for anything that would give her a moment's advantage.

Her fingers finally gripped her salvation, a tiny bottle of pepper spray that Devon had given her a few weeks back. She'd thought it was ridiculous at the time, but if she got out of this, she was certain she would kiss him for his part in her escape.

She quickly slammed her eyes shut as she sent a burst of the pepper spray over her right shoulder in the direction of her attacker, feeling the burn against her own skin as well.

The moment she felt his fingers open slightly, she bit down as hard as she could on the hand covering her mouth and flung her head back towards his face. He fell backwards as her skull connected with his and she quickly flung herself towards the turnstiles and out towards the street in the hopes that a car or a taxi might stop for her. Her only hope was that the man wouldn't pursue her with witnesses.

Her eyes burned slightly from the pepper spray, but she knew it was nothing compared to her attacker's pain.

When she hit the curb, a taxi screeched to a halt with the horn blaring as she fell into the street. Her knees burned as the pavement bit into her skin, but her hands stopped the forward momentum as she reached out for the hood of the cab.

She pushed off with her left hand and ran to the door, all but throwing herself into the seat, only looking back towards her attacker after the door had closed and she slammed the lock in place. He had receded into the shadows again as she let her lungs release the breath she'd been holding.

The cab driver impatiently asked her where she was headed until he flipped on the vanity lights and saw the dark streaks of mascara on her cheeks. Blood had stained her hair an odd shade of pink and it was matted to the right side of her head. He could see the terror in her eyes.

"Miss, are you all right? Do you need me to take you to a hospital? Or call the police?" he asked.

"No, I'm okay. Can you just take me to Fullerton and Western?" she said as she choked back the sob that was trying to escape.

"Okay, miss. Are you sure you don't need a hospital?" he questioned as he pulled away from the curb.

"I'm sure. I'll call a friend," she whispered as she pulled her phone from her pocket.

"I really think we should call the cops," the cabbie protested.

She ignored the man and skimmed through her phone, looking for the number of the only person she could think to call at two in the morning. She knew he'd come for her, and at the moment, she just wanted someone to make her feel safe.

The phone rang three times before he answered, his voice huskier than she was accustomed to, as he had undoubtedly been asleep.

"Dev," she said with relief clear in her tone.

"Molly, it's two in the morning; is everything okay?" he asked, sounding a bit annoyed and just a bit concerned.

"No," she answered as the first tear fell.

"No? You're not okay?" he asked, sounding decidedly more alert.

"Please, can you come and get me?" she asked.

"Where?" he asked without a moment of hesitation.

"My apartment. Fullerton and Western," she told him.

"Okay, but you're going to have to tell me what the hell is going on when I get there."

Devon became concerned when she didn't answer, until he heard her whisper in the background, "Would you mind just sitting here until my friend gets here? You can keep the meter running."

"Molly, I'm on my way. Sit tight," he said as started to hang up.

"Wait!" she wailed before he could hang up the phone. "Please, can you just stay on the phone?"

Devon was starting to freak out a bit at the panic that clung to her every word when she made that request.

"Okay, Mol. I'll stay on the line. Just do me a favor and keep talking to me. I'm going to put you on speaker phone, okay?"

"Okay," she whispered, sounding a tiny bit more relaxed.

"Are you hurt?" he asked as he pulled on a pair of jeans and a sweatshirt.

"A little," she said quietly.

"What's a little, sweetheart? Do you need to go to the hospital?" he asked.

"No! Not until you get here." She cried as she wrapped her left arm around her legs, clutching her right to her chest, and stared out the window towards her apartment building. She continued to stare at the road ahead of them, the road she knew Devon would be coming down shortly.

She heard his car start and she let go of the breath she'd been holding, knowing he would be there soon.

"Please. Drive fast," she whispered to him.

Devon had never heard Molly sound like she did in that moment. She worried for her friends like anyone would, but she was always headstrong and self-assured. At the moment, she sounded like a mewling kitten and that scared the crap out of him.

Molly heard the sirens in the distance and finally let go of the emotions she'd been trying so hard to keep reined in. Her eyes flooded with tears as the adrenaline finally slipped away and the very real consequences of her encounter were allowed to sink in. She could have been badly hurt, or worse. She knew it could have been much worse.

One of the downsides of having a diner full of cops all day, thanks to Dev and Mase, there were always lots of stories.

"I'm almost there, Mol, can you hear the sirens?" he asked.

She didn't answer him; she had quickly spiraled into hysterical sobs that shook her small frame almost as soon as she knew that the danger had truly passed.

"Miss, are you sure you're okay? Maybe I should flag down this cop?" the cabbie wondered as he saw the flashing lights up ahead. He took the phone from her hand just as he heard the man on the other end.

"I am that cop," Devon shouted, hoping the driver would hear him as he hopped out of his car, which was in a tow-away zone, but he didn't care. He figured either they'd run the plate and see it was his, or they'd ticket him and he honestly didn't give a crap at the moment. All he cared about was getting to Molly.

"Okay, sir. She's in my cab," the cabbie answered as he flashed his lights to signal the man heading towards them.

Molly had tucked her chin to her knees and continued to stare out the window towards the intersection ahead. When she saw him, she leaned her forehead to her knees.

She heard the front door open, assuming the driver had stepped out. She could hear the cabbie talking to Dev, though she couldn't understand what was being said.

A moment later, the door opened behind her and she heard Dev speak in a soothing voice. "Look at me, sweetheart. Let me see you."

He watched as her shoulders shook violently and carefully lifted his hand towards her cheek.

"Please. Look at me. Tell me what happened," he pleaded.

When she still didn't look at him, he gently turned her face in his direction instantly noticing a streak of blood matted into her hair and drying against her skin, which was noticeably paler than was normal. His heart began thumping out a steady beat as fear crested over the surface.

He let his thumb gently travel over her cheekbone until he saw the source of the bleeding. He let his hand slide down her back as he whispered in her ear, "Put your arms around my neck."

The moment she raised her arms, she recoiled in pain, pulling them protectively back against her body. That was when Dev saw the wound on her arm. He was certain that the color had drained from his skin now as well when he realized just how much blood had soaked through her clothing.

"Shit, Molly. We need to get to the hospital," Devon told her as he slid into the seat beside her. The cab driver grabbed a clean towel from the trunk and handed it to Devon as soon as he saw the wound and Devon carefully wrapped it around her arm. Molly whimpered as he wrapped the towel around her arm.

The cab driver moved back behind the wheel, glancing in the rearview mirror and noticing the concern etched on the young man's face.

"We'll be there in a few minutes. Hopefully, none of your buddies pull me over," the cabbie said, trying to lighten the mood.

"Keep driving. If they do, I won't let them give you a ticket, and it will help us get there faster," he said as he pressed the towel more firmly over her arm in an effort to stop the bleeding.

She yelped in pain, and his heart broke, knowing he was the cause.

"I'm sorry, sweetheart. I didn't mean to hurt you, but we need to get the bleeding under control," he crooned as he pressed his lips to her forehead, feeling the cool, damp sweat that covered her skin.

"Listen, my friend, I'm going to give you my card. Call me and I'll cover the steam cleaning. I'm afraid you're going to need it," Devon told the cabbie, sliding his card through the slot after glancing at the back seat.

"When I saw her dart out in front of my cab, I knew that something terrible had happened. I'm just glad that I was there when she needed an escape."

"Thank you. Not everyone would have stopped," he whispered.

"I have a daughter a couple years younger than her. She is a freshman in college. I would like to think someone might stop and help her if she ever needed it," the cabbie said before re-focusing on his route.

"I'm going to call Mase and Dakota, okay?" he whispered.

She nodded as he pulled out her phone, which the cabbie had handed him earlier.

"Molly?" Mason asked in confusion, his voice rough, as he'd clearly been awoken from a sound sleep.

"It's Dev."

Before he could get a word out, Mason spoke up. "You could have waited until morning to tell us you finally caved."

"What? No! I'm in a cab with Molly. We're on our way to the hospital."

"What! Are you okay? What happened? Is Molly okay?" Mason rattled off.

Devon heard Dakota's soft voice in the background, undoubtedly worried by Mason's outburst.

"I'm fine, but Molly was attacked tonight."

"What hospital?" Mason asked as his phone beeped in his ear. A moment later, it pinged again with a new voicemail. That would have to wait.

"Saint Mary's?" Devon asked the cabbie, who nodded in confirmation. "Saint Mary's," he repeated to his brother.

"We're on our way," Mason said. "She's going to be okay, isn't she?"

"Yeah." Devon said, sounding less than convinced as he watched the blood begin to soak through the towel.

Mason heard Devon whisper, "I'm sorry sweetheart; I know this hurts, but I need to apply more pressure."

Her scream echoed in his ears as he disconnected the call and threw his clothes on. Dakota walked out of the closet with her cane in hand and fully dressed a few seconds later, giving their address over the phone. He knew there would be no dissuading her from being there for her friend.

When she hung up, she started to move towards the door carefully until she felt his hand wrap around her elbow, expecting an argument over her accompanying him to the hospital.

Shock registered briefly as he simply said, "How long until the cab gets here?"

"Five minutes," she answered as he led her down the stairs.

As they waited in the front foyer, Mason's phone rang again, reminding him of the missed call from earlier.

"Mason Cole," he answered.

"Mase. I just got a call; there was a murder near the Blue Line stop at California. Taber said he tried to call you, but went straight to voicemail," Piper said.

"Can you grab Mel and head over there? I'm on my way to Saint Mary's to meet Dev."

"Is he okay?" Piper asked, his voice laced with concern.

"Yeah. Molly was attacked. I don't know anything beyond that, but I'll let you know as soon as I do," Mason offered.

"Okay, call me as soon as you know anything. Mel and I can handle this," Piper said as he hung up and dialed Melinda.

When she answered, Piper explained the case first, waiting until he picked her up to share the reason behind Mase and Dev's absence knowing it would slow her down. He was happy to have her back after she'd been laid up for two months following her recovery from a stab wound on the "Reaper" case. They all knew she had been extremely lucky. Mason's ability to keep calm under the direst of circumstances had likely been the only reason she was standing on the sidewalk waiting impatiently when Piper pulled up.

"So what are we looking at?" she asked.

Piper explained what Taber had told him about the case and quickly followed that up with what he knew about Molly in hopes of stopping the onslaught of commentary she was getting ready to fire off about Mason and Devon's absence.

He'd anticipated her train of thought since this had been one of the rare occasions one or both of the brothers weren't on the scene since they'd started working together. The pair never missed an opportunity harass Piper, or Melinda for that matter, with regard to late arrivals.

"You don't know anything?" she asked in disbelief.

"No. Mase hasn't seen her yet, and Dev isn't answering his phone at all," Piper shared as he pulled up to the curb behind a squad car.

"Tell me what you know," Melinda said to the officer.

"Looked like an assault that ended in homicide, but there's something rather odd about it," the officer said as he led them to the tarp under the stairwell just beyond the turnstiles.

"I assume that's why we got called in?" Piper wondered aloud as he lifted the edge of the tarp not at all prepared for what he saw. In front of him lay a woman in her early twenties with blonde hair, fair skin, maybe five and a half feet tall.

"God, she could be Molly's twin," Melinda said, just as Piper's thoughts had wandered in a similar direction.

www.ingramcontent.com/pod-product-compliance
Lightning Source LLC
Chambersburg PA
CBHW071201260626
47162CB00003B/1128